When another head is found in Blood Pond, Detective August Greystone must try to keep his own head while searching for the killer. All this time, August and his lover Bruce Monkton have tried to put the past behind them and build a secure and happy future as a couple, only to be brutally reminded of the terrible circumstances that initially brought them together.

With few clues and even fewer witnesses, August feels like a fish out of water, trying to deal with the memories of his own brother's murder years earlier. Bruce's assertion that someone is after him also weighs heavily on his mind, making August wonder if Bruce is actually insane after all.

Questions never truly answered resurface along with the boy's head in Blood Pond. Is a serial killer still on the prowl hunting for fresh victims, or has the murderous psychopath been at August's side, and sharing his bed all along?

This book has been previously published previously some and has won many awards.

Blood Pond Resurfacing
Copyright © 2019 D.J. Manly
ISBN: 978-1-4874-2492-3
Cover art by Martine Jardin

Published by eXtasy Books Inc or
Devine Destinies, an imprint of eXtasy Books Inc

Look for us online at:
www.eXtasybooks.com or www.devinedestinies.com

Blood Pond Resurfacing
Blood Pond, Book 2

By

D.J. Manly

DEDICATION

To my readers . . .

CHAPTER NINE

August drove at an even seventy miles an hour along the road to Blood Pond, his hands cradling the steering wheel in an iron grip, his focus on the road straight ahead. The more distance he covered, the more he wondered if he'd be able to pry his hands loose when the time came. Maybe he'd be stuck there in the car, frozen in time, clutching that wheel like an anchor.

He hadn't said anything to Bruce after he'd received the phone call. He'd just kind of gone into automatic, strapping on his gun holster, like he would have when called out on any routine homicide. A kind of numbness came over him, his mind a fog, the pain resting just under the surface waiting for the ideal time to float to the surface and paralyze him.

As the cottage country came into view, he swallowed something hard in his throat. He'd grown up here, among the trees and the water. He and Tommy had spent all those warm summer days at Blood Pond, frolicking in the pond, never suspecting of course that one day it would be the place his brother's head would end up.

He could almost hear his brother's laughter, that crazy, zany laugh he had that would light up his eyes. God, he missed him so much. They'd been close, even though August was five years older. He remembered how Tommy used to like to run and jump on him whenever August was on the sofa. They'd wrestle, and August would tickle him. When Tommy was a toddler, he'd eventually curl up in Au-

1

gust's lap and fall asleep, with his thumb in his mouth. When he got older, he still liked to jump on him, especially when August was fast asleep, and initiate a wrestling contest.

Tears stung his eyes, and his vision blurred for a moment then cleared. He'd never really forgiven himself for missing Tommy's sixteenth birthday. It wasn't that he thought the therapists were telling him bullshit when they insisted that it wasn't his fault. It was true he wasn't a genie. He didn't have ESP. He couldn't have known that Tommy was going to be abducted by a psycho and murdered. But still, he'd never stopped wondering if he had come home for his brother's birthday, maybe they would have been together the whole time, and Tommy would have been safe.

As he drove around the bend, the illumination of flashing lights lit up his windshield. Police cars were parked beside the water, half hidden behind the sparsely wooded area on the right side of the road. Three minutes more and he'd be right on top of them.

His stomach heaved a little. His heart had started beating just a little bit harder back at the hotel, and now the pain in his head was intense, moving down his shoulders, even radiating into his arms. If he didn't know himself, he would have thought he was in cardiac arrest, but he knew this was how his body reacted to extreme stress.

He was thinking about Bruce as he drew up alongside one of the police cruisers. He was sure Bruce, too, must be feeling it. He felt a pang of guilt about the way he'd reacted after getting the call. Bruce had wanted to talk, but August just couldn't. He knew they'd talk about it later. In fact, that's probably all they'd talk about for a very long time to come unless Bruce went into his shell.

Bruce could close himself off, not talk to him for hours, or even days sometimes. It's just the way he was. Doctors hypothesized that this behavior was probably the result of losing his twin, but they didn't know for sure. August knew that had something to do with it, but there was more. The life Bruce had led, the secrecy and the psychological pain had taken its toll on him. It was a wonder Bruce was sane at all.

Most doctors had never known a case where identical twins could communicate telepathically with each other like Bruce and Clay had. But there had been a lot of evidence and studies which suggested that twins could read each other's minds in some cases or be hundreds of miles apart and still buy the exact same pair of shoes.

August climbed out of the car, zeroing in on Desmond Johnson, the Whitefield chief of police, who was deep in conversation with two of his officers. They stood in front of one of the squad cars. There was another parked behind it and an ambulance.

The three Whitefield police officers met him halfway.

"August," Desmond said, smiling, holding out his hand, "long time no see. I didn't even know you were in town until all this."

August took his hand. "Short visit."

They'd been lovers once, briefly, more than ten years back when they were both in the academy. Desmond was an ambitious cop, would have moved to the big city if his chance for promotion in Whitefield hadn't been such a given. His father had been the chief of police of a nearby town. Desmond was all about appearances, deep in the closet, but basically a decent sort of guy and an intuitive cop.

"Were you planning on stopping by?" He sounded a little hurt.

"I would have gotten around to it," August told him, although he was sure Bruce wouldn't have liked it much.

Bruce had a jealous streak that August really didn't consider to be one of his attractive features.

Desmond looked apologetic. "Heard you were on a kind of vacation. Sorry to have to break it up. Boys . . ." He turned to his men who were standing just behind Desmond, looking like they, were bursting at the seams. "This is Detective Greystone from Manchester, an old friend of mine."

August nodded at them. "How you doin'?"

"We're real pleased to meet you," one of them said with a big smile, shaking August's hand a little too hard. The other smiled too and basically parroted his companion, extending his hand as well.

He understood their enthusiasm. They were small-town cops whose usual routine consisted of writing out parking tickets. This was their chance to do what they were really trained for. "Where is it?" August asked, looking past them.

"Coroner isn't here yet." Desmond motioned, and the four men walked down the road to a little embankment that led to the pond. "Had to wake the guy out of a dead sleep," Desmond informed him.

August's gaze shot to the tree on his right. The last time he'd been to Blood Pond, he'd almost died here.

Bruce's twin had tied him to that tree.

In front of him now on the ground was a more pressing matter. He reluctantly glanced away from the tree and settled his gaze on the car blanket that covered a lump of something on the ground. This felt fucking surreal.

"I saw your friend, Bruce Monkton, a few times this week." Desmond cleared his throat. "He's some hotshot marketing guy now."

August's gaze never left the blanket. He couldn't help but note how Desmond avoided the word 'partner,' when he spoke of Bruce. "Yes, Bruce has done really well for himself."

"Considering," Desmond added.

August gave him a sharp look.

"We didn't want to touch anything until the evidence people got here," Desmond went on. "I called Manchester right away, of course, that's how I found out you were in town. They told me you've become something of a profiler. Guess you'll be heading up the investigation?"

"That's what I'm told."

"Well, you got all the cooperation here you need, August."

"I appreciate that."

"Must be doing pretty well for yourself, staying at the Mountain View. It's pricy."

Desmond went on about the hotel, but his words weren't really registering. August's attention was now on the two girls who were perched at the back of the ambulance. "Those two girls, they the ones who called it in?"

"You don't miss a trick." Desmond smiled.

"Just the head?" August asked, looking at him.

"So far. We'll send some divers down first thing this morning. Want to take a look at it or . . ."

His stomach heaved a little. His brother's face flashed in front of his eyes. "I'll wait for forensics. Got an ID on the victim?"

"Yep." One of the officers stepped forward. He flipped open his pad and began to read. "Name is Dennis Jameson, fifteen, reported missing three days ago. He attended the local high school, played on the basketball team. I saw the kid play. He had promise. His parents own the local flower shop here in town. They moved here three years ago."

"Anyone new hanging around town this last week that you know about?" August looked at Desmond. "Guests at the hotels, the campgrounds?"

"Haven't had time to check it all," Desmond said. "We'll get on it. The only one I can think of offhand is Bruce." He met August's gaze.

'There was a fucking conference, Des. Surely there were people from out of town here."

"We'll check." He nodded and looked away.

August walked back up the embankment. The cop with the pad followed. "What are two young girls like that doing at Blood Pond at this time of night?"

"Skinny dipping," the cop said with a toothy smile.

"They're ah . . ." He lowered his voice. "You know, queer?"

August raised an eyebrow. "You mean lesbians perhaps?" He sighed.

"Yeah, that, what you said, fun to watch on video." He chuckled.

"Look," August told him, ignoring the remark, "I can handle this on my own, ah . . ."

"Bob, Bob Smithson, sir. And I heard about that case you solved up in the city, the one with the grandfather guy who was molesting the boys on the baseball team. I'm a big admirer of your work."

"Thanks, Bob." He reached out his hand. "Can you give me your notes, please?"

"Be pleased to." He passed them over. "You need me, detective, you holler," he said. "I'll be right there before you can say two birds in a tree."

August kept walking. "I'll remember that."

Two ambulance technicians stood at the back of the ambulance chatting as August approached. The young women were huddled together with blankets around their shoulders. August smiled at them.

The medics, two men, nodded at him and walked away. "Hello, ladies," he said. "Are you alright?"

One nodded, the other murmured "yes." They'd both been crying.

"I'm Detective Greystone. You can call me August." He glanced at the pad he'd taken from Bob.

They looked back at him silently.

"I realize this must be a shock. I know you've already spoken with the officers over there, but could you please answer a few questions for me?"

One of them was plump with long dark hair. The blonde looked like she could have been a fashion model. They were both pretty and no more than seventeen or eighteen.

"Did you know the victim?"

"Penny did," the dark-haired girl said. "I've seen him around."

"I see." August looked at Penny, his voice gentle. "Do you remember when you last saw Dennis?"

"My brother," she began, "played basketball with him on Wednesday."

Was he in school at all this week?"

"I don't know. You'd have to ask Peter."

"That's your brother?"

She nodded.

"Did they play basketball here at the school or did they play at another school?"

"They played at another school."

"Can you tell me exactly what happened tonight?"

"We're in deep shit." The dark-haired girl sighed, chewing her nail.

August checked the pad. "Why is that, ah . . . Francine?"

"We're not supposed to be up here together."

Penny looked at August. "We're not allowed to be friends."

August nodded. "I see. Okay, well, you came up here anyway, right, against your parents' wishes?"

They both nodded.

"And you went swimming in Blood Pond?"

"Yeah," Francine said.

"What time was that about?"

"About . . . ah, two hours ago," Penny said.

"So, let's say about," August checked his watch.

"Eight-thirty."

"That would be about right," Francine said.

Did you see anyone around?"

No, and we made sure," the blonde said. "We, ah . . . swam naked." She blushed.

"I see," August said. "And which of you saw the . . . body part?"

"Me first," Penny choked out. The tears rolled down her face. Francine put an arm around her. "I just looked down, and I saw . . . I saw . . ."

"Take your time," August said. "You saw what?"

"These two dead eyes just staring at me." She lowered her head and started to cry again.

August nodded toward Francine. "You stay with her, okay? I assume someone called your parents?"

Francine nodded as she pulled Penny into her embrace.

August looked around to see headlights coming toward him in the distance.

Desmond came walking over. "Coroner is here," he announced.

"Fine." His cell phone was ringing. "Excuse me. I'll be right there."

"August," the gruff voice said on the other end of the phone. It was Captain Affleck in Manchester. "You hooked up with that case in Whitefield yet?"

"I'm at the scene now."

"Good. You know I want you heading up this one."

"Yes, sir."

"I want you to stay down there until you find this bastard. I'm sending you people. We need results on this one."

August narrowed his eyes. Captain Affleck answered his question in the next sentence.

"The victim is the grandson of some hot shot politician in Washington, a senator."

"I see. Well, the killing fits the MO of—"

"You're not going to get weird on this one, are you, August?"

"Weird?"

"You know, because of Tommy?"

"No," he said then gritted his teeth, "but there is a possibility that it could be this guy, that he has resurfaced and—"

"Could be. Anything is possible. It's true these bastards can pop up again after years of hibernation. But I thought that one was dead."

"No hard evidence to back up that fact."

"Right, well, I'll send you whoever you need, okay? But right now, you're the best profiler we got. We'll pay your expenses but not at the Mountain View. Got you registered at the Travel Lodge for an indeterminate period.'

"Damn," August muttered, "am I being demoted?" It was a joke, but Affleck had never been much of a joker.

"Forensics should be there by now. Have Alice give me a shout when she arrives."

"Is she booked at the luxurious Travel Lodge too?"

"Smart, Greystone. Okay, make use of Johnson, too, when you're down there. His guys can do the legwork for routine stuff. Those Whitefield cops should be good for something besides eating doughnuts."

"Gotcha," he said, glad Desmond hadn't heard that remark. He knew that urban snobbism existed, but it was still a little shocking to hear it in plain English.

The coroner was a short, stocky little African-American man with a bizarre sense of humor. Desmond introduced them, and August braced himself for when the coroner peeled away the blanket.

"Looks like someone lost his head," Markus Zamziane announced with a big grin. "We need for him to find the rest of himself." He looked at Desmond.

"We're working on that."

August forced himself to look down at what was left of the young boy.

"Hasn't been in the water that long," Zamziane said. "I'd say three days, no more." He looked at August. "Clean cut, probably some kind of a long sword. Maybe the killer was Sir Lancelot." He laughed at his own joke.

Desmond's phone rang, and he walked away.

August breathed a sigh of relief when Zamziane covered the bloody head back up. "Thanks."

"I'd like to say it was a pleasure . . . but . . ."

"Forensics team is in town," Desmond called out. "They're lost. I'm going to meet them and lead them here."

August nodded. His stomach felt queasy. He'd seen plenty of dead bodies and body parts before. Usually, he could handle it, but all he thought about when he saw what once the animated face of a young boy had been, was that Tommy must have looked like this when the police found him.

Zamziane was staring at him.

"Excuse me," August said, and walked up the ravine to the road. He took a few breaths. Someone came over and asked him if he was alright.

His cell phone rang again. He hesitated then put the phone to his ear. "Yeah."

"August, are you alright?"

"Fine. You?"

"I was worried. Did you find out anything? Who is it?"

"A local boy from town. Two girls found him. He's got a big shot granddaddy down in Washington."

Silence.

10

"Look, I'm going to be stuck here for a while. They're going to transfer me to the Lodge. You going home?"

"I can stay around another day then I should get back to the office. Honey, maybe you should get off this thing, let someone else do this."

"I'm a homicide detective, Bruce. This is a homicide."

"I know but—"

"Get some sleep. I'll be there as soon as I can."

The sun had already risen when August drove around the lake back toward town, and despite the sun, the sky looked doubtful about what direction it would take for the remainder of the day. He'd hung around until forensics finished up, and he'd spoken to the girls' parents, who frankly seemed more concerned about their daughters hanging out together than they did about a boy's head being in the pond. People were strange.

As he pulled into town, he spotted Alice Comeau standing outside the town diner. He checked his watch. Place wouldn't open for a little while yet.

Alice, or Al, as she was more commonly called, was working homicide when he returned to the job four years ago. They'd collaborated on a few cases. Then she got interested in the scientific end of things and ended up going back to school. Now she worked forensics. She was an attractive woman around thirty, athletic and tough, with dark wavy hair. She was one hell of a cop too, but she didn't have much luck with men. She'd already been divorced twice. It was a running joke in the department.

When Alice saw him, she waved.

He pulled over to the curb and grinned at her. "Hungry?"

"When in the hell is breakfast in this one-horse town anyway?" She grinned at him then looked back at the diner.

"Opens at eight, Al, usually, if you're lucky."

"Hell, another hour. I'm starved."

"Get in," he said. "I'll give you some gum to chew."

She walked around and got into the passenger side, laughing. "Want a smoke?"

"Yeah, I want a smoke, but I quit, remember?"

"Wish I could. How did you do it?

"I suffered," he replied.

"I won't smoke," she said, stuffing her pack back into the pocket of her windbreaker.

"It's okay. Open the window. It won't bother me."

She shook her head. "Trying to kill me off, eh, Gus? Forget it; I'll suffer, too." She paused then gave him a meaningful look. "How are you doing anyway?"

"I'm doing," he sighed, laying his head back against the headrest. He was tired, but he knew even if he went back to the hotel, he wouldn't be able to sleep.

She reached out and stroked his hair for a second then quickly withdrew. "If you asked to be taken off this case, no one would blame you, you know?"

He lifted his head, peering at her. "Funny, Bruce practically said the same thing a little while ago. I don't want to be off this case."

"Okay."

"Look, there is no evidence that Clay killed his accomplice. He might have told Bruce that, but it doesn't mean it was true."

"How is Bruce?" She looked out the passenger window.

He almost expected her to spit when she said his name. She'd never liked him, although he knew she tried hard to hide it. "Fine."

That bitch hates me. She wants you between her thighs, that's why.

He hated it when Bruce talked like that. Bruce had told him that one night after they'd come home from a retirement party for one of the big brass in the department. It was the first time he'd met Alice. August didn't believe it for a minute, and it really bothered him how possessive and jealous Bruce could get. Bruce was frail in his own way and insecure, and so usually August put it down to that and let it go.

"Johnson told me he was in town all week," Alice said, bringing August back to the present.

"Who?"

"Bruce."

"A lot of people were in this town all week, Al." He gave her a meaningful look.

"I know but . . . given his connection with all this stuff . . ." She sighed. "You do know that he's being considered a suspect."

"A suspect? That's ridiculous."

"Desmond Johnson told me. Bruce shouldn't leave town just yet."

"You've got to be fucking kidding me."

She put up a hand. "Don't shoot the messenger. If you ask me, Desmond Johnson is a bit of a Rambo, not to mention that he's in love with you. That doesn't help."

August's mouth dropped open.

"Oh, don't act so surprised, August. It's obvious that you banged the poor salivating dope back at the academy. You did go to the academy together, didn't you?"

August made a face. "Ancient history."

"For you, maybe."

"I need to talk to him about Bruce. He's way out of line."

"Look, August, you know that usually, I've got your back. Hell, we were partners. But, on this one, I'm afraid I agree with him."

"What? I can't believe you. Bruce was cleared of everything after his brother was shot."

She nodded quietly. "His mother still up in the pen doing

time?"

"Yeah."

"Does Bruce see her?"

"No. He wants nothing to do with her."

"It was a strange case. Clay was kept in the basement because he was unstable, but his mother said he could cause her to have headaches if she didn't do as he said. Personally, I never bought that one. Even Bruce claimed that Clay could speak to him in his mind."

"There have been a lot of studies on identical twins, Al. Anything is possible."

"Why did the mother protect the bad one? Why didn't she admit him to the hospital? She claims to this day that Bruce was the sick one, not Clay."

"She wants revenge against Bruce for testifying against her, that's all."

"Um . . ."

"Okay, what? Out with it."

"Nothing. Just Bruce hung out with your brother, fell for him, but Tommy was straight, not interested, and suddenly, his twin emerges from the basement, lures a serial killer here and takes them both hostage? The killer never touches Bruce though, not to mention that Bruce takes off and leaves town when he escapes instead of going to the police."

August looked at her. "It looks like you've spent some time reading the files. Bruce was in shock, terrified."

"But he knew Clay was involved."

"Not at the time. He was confused."

"Tell me what you remember after Clay took you to Blood Pond."

"What for?"

"Just to appease me."

"Okay." He sighed. "Clay came to my house, knocked me out and took me to Blood Pond. He tied me to a tree, and I

14

assume meant to kill me. He almost did. If it hadn't been for Bruce, I'd be dead. He went there to Blood Pond and tackled Clay. They fell into the pond and then, instead of leaving Clay, Bruce pulled him out. He'd been shot."

"How did Clay get you to Blood Pond alone? I've seen Bruce. He and Clay must have been around the same size."

August nodded.

"You're a big guy, August, tall, muscular. Do you think someone of that stature could have carried you to Blood Pond? Was there ever a vehicle found?"

"What are you saying?"

"I'm saying I doubt he could have done it alone."

"So, Bruce helped him? Is that what you are trying to say? Al, if Bruce wanted me dead, don't you think he would have found a way to do it by now? We sleep in the same bed for Christ's sake."

"I never said that Bruce wanted you dead. I truly think he loves you. But Bruce and Clay had an unusual bond, August. I think it was wrapped up all too neatly. After Bruce called you, after he'd supposedly stopped Clay from killing you, you went to find them, right?"

"Yeah."

"Someone came out of the barn when you got there, and you knew it was Clay."

"He was wearing boots."

"Were they dressed exactly alike? The twins?"

"Similar. Jeans, Clay had a coat. Bruce was wearing a couple of layers of clothes. He didn't own a coat, and he had on running shoes."

"Other than that, could you tell them apart? Was it dark?"

"Fairly dark; it was the middle of winter, early evening." He hesitated. He knew where she was going.

Al looked at him. "August . . ." She touched his hand, her voice growing softer as she met his gaze. "Did you ever think that maybe you shot the wrong twin?"

When Bruce heard the key in the lock, he jumped up from where he was sitting on the loveseat and ran to open the door. August walked into the hotel room and closed the door. Bruce wanted to hug him, to kiss him, but he knew August wasn't in the mood. He unsnapped his holster, walked across the room, and slid his gun into the nightstand beside the bed.

"You look tired," Bruce said.

August hadn't spoken a word yet. He turned around now and stared at him, just stared at him as if he'd never seen him before.

"What? Why are you looking at me like that?"

August slumped down on the side of the bed. "I'm tired, so tired."

Bruce moved closer. "Did anyone see anything?"

August shook his head. "Two young girls found the . . ." He didn't bother finishing his sentence.

"How awful."

"Bruce," August said, looking up at him, "do you love me?"

Bruce sucked in some breath. Love him? August was his life. He'd never loved anyone the way he loved this man. Tears filled his eyes. "Of course I love you." He shook his head.

August rubbed his face. "Last night felt surreal, like I might be losing my mind, like everything we thought was behind us has come back."

"No." Bruce came to sit beside him now. "No, August. This has nothing to do with us."

August took Bruce by the shoulders and gave him a firm shake. "It has everything to do with us. It has—"

The sound of rapping on the door caused August to abruptly release him. Bruce was frightened of that look in his eyes, wild and almost vacant. "I'll get the door." Bruce got up from the bed and crossed the room. August followed him.

Desmond Johnson stood there with that apologetic look on his face, Joe by his side. "Hello, Mr. Monkton," he said then looked over Bruce's shoulder. "Hello, August."

Can I talk to you outside a moment?" August asked between clenched teeth.

"You can, but it won't change anything," Desmond said. "I have to do this."

Bruce looked at August then back at the two cops who stood at the door. "What's going on?"

"Nothing," August replied angrily. "Desmond, this isn't going to happen."

"It's routine, August. We have to question anyone who's come into town this past week."

Bruce placed a hand on August's arm. "It's okay. I've got nothing to hide." He stood back and opened the door wider. "Come in."

"We won't hold you up long," Desmond said.

"Get on with it," August grunted.

"So, Bruce . . ." Desmond said. "You don't mind if I call you Bruce, do you?"

"Not at all," Bruce said, inviting Desmond and the other officer to sit down.

They declined. Desmond snapped open a writing pad. "So, I understand that you gave a conference here at the convention center on marketing strategies."

"That's right. Three days."

"And you were the only speaker, right?"

"Yes."

"And you were at the Travel Lodge on your own all

week."

"Yes. I came here to the Mountain View last night with August."

Desmond Johnson didn't comment. He wouldn't.

I know you'd love to find something on me, be able to comfort my lover as they take me away. Sorry, you won't find a damn thing, and you won't get the chance to get August into your bed again. I'll make sure of that.

Bruce smiled, waiting for Desmond's next question.

Desmond smiled back, but Bruce knew it was forced.

"After the conference . . . It, ah, lasted three days?"

"That's right."

"What did you do in the evenings?"

"I went back to the hotel, not this one as you know, the Lodge at the end of town, but I've said that, haven't I? This place was a gift from August, a little romantic getaway for both of us."

"Every evening you were alone at the Lodge?" The officer with him suddenly piped up.

"Yes."

"Can you verify that?" Desmond inquired without changing gears.

"Well, no. I was alone."

"You ate alone?"

Yes. I took stuff back to the room, take-out mostly."

"And you never stepped outside, never went for a walk, to a bar?" Desmond asked.

"Look, if he said he didn't, he didn't," August interjected. He stood leaning against the wall. So far, he'd been silent, but Bruce knew he was having a tough time staying that way.

"They were long days," Bruce said. "I had stuff to prepare for the following day, and I went to bed early."

"What time?" Desmond asked.

"Ten maybe."

"Alone?"

"Okay," August snapped, "that's enough."

Bruce held up his hand. "It's alright, sweetheart. Yes," he told Desmond, "alone. If you knew a man like August would soon be in your bed, would you sleep with someone else and run the risk of losing him?"

Desmond snapped the book shut.

There, you bastard. I got you that time.

"Look, Mr. Monkton," Desmond fixed him with his gaze, "I'm going to come right out and say it. You're not to leave town until—"

"That's enough." August moved forward. "You're going to leave before I throw you out of here."

"August," Desmond complained, "you're not being objective here. We need to—"

"I'm heading up this investigation, and I'll tell you what we need to do. Right now, I need to sleep. We'll talk about this later."

Desmond nodded. "Come on, Joe," he said to the other guy. He nodded at Bruce, and the two men left.

August slammed the door shut and locked it.

"I expected that he'd take this opportunity to jump down my throat. He just loved the power he had over the guy you're fucking."

August made a face. "This isn't about that."

"Yes, it is," Bruce said. "You fucked him a few times, and he thinks you belong to him."

"Oh, Bruce, grow up."

"Grow up? Do you think it helps that he's your ex?"

"He's not my ex." August took off his shirt.

"Well, he can't have you. He'll just have to accept that."

"Bruce, Christ." August turned and glared at him. "You are a fucking suspect; don't you get it?"

Bruce sobered. Suspect? Why in hell would he be a suspect? He followed August into the bathroom, watching while he took off the rest of his clothes and turned on the shower. "I didn't do anything," Bruce said.

"Your brother did," August replied. "Your brother murdered mine."

Bruce sucked in some breath. "A serial killer murdered Tommy."

"A serial killer lured here by Clay, manipulated by him, tailor-made to kill my brother because you had a crush on him."

"Clay is dead and so is that monster."

"Are they? Are they dead?"

Bruce reached out and braced himself against the wall. "What? What in hell are you saying?"

August articulated each word. "You heard me. Are they dead?"

"Clay killed the . . . He buried him under the cabin and—"

"There was never any proof of that, no proof that a serial killer ever existed or that Clay killed him. No remains. How fucking convenient."

"You know there was another one. I told you there was. I was there, not you," Bruce retorted angrily.

"Could have been Clay."

"I told you, there were two, Clay and another man. It was the man who was—"

"The man in the mask, I know, I know. You never saw his face. The only fucking thing you remember is a tattoo of a dragon on his forearm."

"Where is all this coming from? That ex-boyfriend of yours putting all this bullshit in your head?"

"He is not my ex-boyfriend." August sighed. "I only had sex with him a few times, and it was nothing to write home about. Stop fucking calling him my boyfriend." August stepped into the shower.

Bruce leaned back against the wall. He closed his eyes. This was hell; hell had returned, threatening to burn them both up in the fire. He stood there, watching August through the transparent curtain, his gaze following the lines of his body. He remembered the first time he'd seen a picture of August. August was dressed in his police uniform, so handsome, so strong and in control. August had always made him feel so safe, so protected.

He stripped off his t-shirt and undid his jeans. He wasn't wearing any socks or underwear. He needed a shower. He needed August.

Bruce moved the curtain aside and stepped into the shower behind August.

August glanced around at him in surprise.

Bruce placed his arms around him, settling his cheek against his back.

"What are you doing?" August demanded as Bruce moved his hand down to fold around August's cock.

"I want you."

"You've got to be kidding." August pushed his hand away and reached over and turned off the shower.

"I really need you, August. I need to be close to you now."

August whipped aside the curtain and reached for a towel. "Sometimes you fucking blow me away. I can't believe," he said, wiping the water off his face and his chest, "that you can be so insensitive."

"Insensitive?" Bruce gawked at him. "I'm not being insensitive."

"You're threatened by Desmond, although I have no idea why, and you need reassurance. Well, I have no strength for your games, Bruce. I'm exhausted, and I'm emotionally drained. I can't even believe that you'd expect me to do that now."

Bruce bit his bottom lip. *Rejection big time.* "Maybe you don't want me anymore."

August paused before he left the bathroom. "Please, Bruce, don't do this. I can't stroke your ego or anything else right now. Have some mercy. Don't make this about you. This is about that kid in Blood Pond and about what we've both lived through. If that bastard is still out there, I want him."

Bruce stood alone in the shower, shivering. He couldn't lose August. *But you will. No one loves you. Only me. I was the only one, and now I'm gone. First chance he gets, he'll be inside that cop. They'll fuck like two champions, two cops, working closely on this one. Where were you when the blackout happened in New York, brother?*

Bruce gasped, turned on the shower, and got underneath the water. He slowly stroked himself, imagining it was August's hand that touched him. *I love you. You are my everything. I'm going to fuck you all night. I will never betray you with Desmond, no matter how he tries to seduce me.*

Bruce closed his eyes, imagined his lover inside him, and he smiled. It was alright now.

CHAPTER TEN

When August opened his eyes and glanced at his watch on the night table, it said it was two in the afternoon. He'd only slept around five hours. It felt like he had sawdust under his eyelids, and the headache had abated somewhat but wasn't completely gone. "Bruce?" He spoke his name as if he didn't expect there to be an answer, and there wasn't.

He swung his legs over the side of the bed and rubbed his face. He needed to shave, needed to check his messages. His stomach was empty as well. He'd never accepted Al's invitation to breakfast.

He stood, stumbled a little, and spotted his Blackberry lying on the bureau. The message light was flashing. He walked over, picked it up, and waited for his voicemail.

"August, it's Des. We need to talk about Bruce. I don't think you can be objective when it comes—" He pressed delete and moved to the next one.

"Hello, August, Al. You should see the digs over here at the Lodge. I half expected you to be here by now. Give me a call." August pressed in the number and walked over to the window. It was pissing rain. He moved the curtain aside. Bruce's car was still there, parked in the same parking spot.

"Hey, handsome," Alice said into the phone suddenly.

"Hey, yourself. I got some much-needed sleep, but I still feel like crap."

"I know that kind of sleep."

"I'm going to shower, shave, and throw on some clothes. I'll head down your way as soon as I stop to see Des."

"He told me he stopped by this morning."

"He's getting carried away."

"He's just doing his job." She laughed. "With extra motivation."

"Yeah, well, he's going to knock it off."

"What is Bruce saying about all this?"

"Don't know, he's not here, and don't get any ideas; his car still is. He has to go back to Manchester."

"Des might give you a hard time on that one."

"Like hell."

Alice laughed. "See you in how long?"

"An hour?"

"Good, there are some things I think we should look at. Hope you don't mind the suggestion."

"No. I'll get with this, I promise."

"I know it's not easy, August. I still say Affleck is taking advantage here."

"No, I need to do this."

"Okay then, I'll order us in some food."

"Sounds good. See you later."

When Bruce heard a car pull up to the curb in front of the cemetery, he didn't pay much attention. Then someone spoke, and he turned around so quickly he almost lost his balance.

Desmond Johnson stood a few feet away, leaning on his squad car. "Hello, Bruce."

Bruce nodded. "Desmond." His running shoes were sinking into the wet grass. It had been raining hard a little while ago. Now the rain had tapered off to a fine mist.

"Chief Johnson to you. Whatcha doing? Talking to the dead?"

He'd come here to be alone. He thought maybe he should

visit his brother's grave one more time before he left town. "I'm paying my respects."

"Yes. And did you show your respect to Tommy Greystone too?"

"Of course." He met Desmond's gaze. "What do you want?"

"You," he said casually. "I want you, behind bars where you belong, where you should have been all along."

"One has to wonder." Bruce raised his chin. "What it is you want more, me in prison, or August alone."

"It's truly a tossup." He nodded.

"You're not even going to deny it, are you?"

"No. I'm not. Why should I? You and I both want the same thing. We understand one another, don't we?"

"Yes," Bruce said between clenched teeth.

Desmond pointed at him suddenly. "Don't leave town."

"You can't keep me here," Bruce protested. "I have to go back to work. So, unless you have any good, hard evidence to prove I've done something wrong . . ." He paused, then said, "Anyway, I'd think you'd want me gone, to have August all to yourself."

"Again, it's a tossup." He shrugged, getting into the car. "Get rid of you temporarily or permanently? It might be worth having to stomach you hanging all over August for a while longer just to get rid of you for good."

"You know," Bruce snarled, approaching the car, "you really should get over this little schoolboy crush you have on my lover. He doesn't want you, never did, never will."

Desmond glanced at him out the car window, gave him the finger then drove off.

August walked outside into the drizzle and got into his car. He'd been hoping Bruce would return before he left, but he hadn't. He dialed Bruce's cell phone as he put the key in the ignition. Bruce picked up on the third ring. "There you are." August adjusted the rearview mirror and turned on the wipers to clean the windshield.

"Hi."

"Where in hell are you anyway?"

"At the cemetery. I wanted to say goodbye."

"I'm surprised."

"I do take the things you say to heart."

"I need to change hotels and move to the Lodge. Do you want to join me there?"

"Sure, later on."

August paused. "Bruce?"

"What?"

"I'm going to talk to Desmond. Don't worry." No reply.

"Bruce, are you still there?"

"Yeah. I think we have a bad connection."

"I'm sorry about this morning."

"It was insensitive of me. We just handle this stuff differently, that's all. Forget it."

"I love you. I promise I'm all yours tonight. Okay?"

"That's a nice thought. Okay. And I love you, August."

"Maybe we can get together for dinner."

"Sounds good. Call me."

"I will."

Ten minutes later, he was parked in front of the Whitefield police station, a red brick building with high cathedral windows and massive white columns on each side of the wide entrance. The building also housed the city hall, and next door to it was the Whitefield fire hall.

Desmond was standing behind the desk when August walked in, discussing something with the dispatcher. He looked up when he saw August. "You got my message then?"

August nodded. "I got it."

"Come into the office." He looked at the young woman. "Hold everything. Give it to Bob if it needs looking after right away."

"Yes, Chief," she said and gave August an appreciative look.

He nodded at her then followed Desmond into his modest office.

Desmond closed the door and went to sit behind the desk. He invited August to take a seat, moving a pile of reports to the side. "Coffee?"

"No, thanks."

"How long have we known each other?" Desmond asked him, leaning back in his office chair.

August sat down. "A long time."

"And do you think I would do anything to hurt you, to cause you undue stress?"

"This isn't about me."

"Jesus Christ, August," he said, "Bruce was up to his neck in this shit. His brother was nuts, and his mother is nuts. If it hadn't been for your testimony, Bruce would have—"

"You can't keep him here in town."

"Yes, I can."

"On what authority?"

"I'm still the chief of police in this town."

"You have to have enough evidence to hold him."

"Suspicion is enough. He was here, and until he showed up, there was no one's head in the pond, August. It's just a coincidence?"

"It's bullshit, Des. You got shit."

"Well, maybe that's gonna change. I got a warrant to search his room and belongings. I'll have it within the hour."

"Fine." August threw up his hands. "Search all you want. You're wasting your time. You won't find anything. He didn't do anything." He stood.

Des shrugged. "Like I said, August, I don't expect you to be objective. You can't be objective when you're fucking his tight little ass every night."

"You're out of line." August yanked open the door. Then he paused and glared back at him. "After you search and find nothing, you won't be able to keep him here."

"One step at a time," Desmond replied, opening a file on his desk. "I may not find anything, but I'm not going to back down on this. I know he's involved."

August walked out. He was fuming with anger when he arrived at the Travel Lodge, a three-story hotel done in white stucco with balconies not large enough to stand on. The rain had stopped, and the sun was out now, but it didn't look as if it could hold out all day. It was going to rain off and on.

Alice was sitting on a small, wooden bench beside the front door of the hotel when he pulled up.

She stood and raised a hand when he got out and took his stuff out of the back seat. She was wearing jeans and an old hooded sweatshirt with her hair tied back. "Oh," she said, studying him, "you're not a happy boy. Someone steal your lollypop?"

"Desmond is getting on my last nerve."

"I'll buy you another," she said with a grin and took his arm.

He laughed a little. "Thanks."

"I've got sandwiches and coffee in the room. I suspect you haven't eaten. You never do when you're ass deep in it. Oh, you're in the room next to mine by the way. I signed in for the department. Remind me to give you your key. I left it in my room."

"Thanks," he said as they walked into the lobby. He didn't have to take time to study the décor. He'd been to these places before. They were basically the same, desk off to the left, two brown leather loveseats parked in the center, bordered by a red oriental rug, and a coffee table in the middle with the daily newspaper and a few magazines thrown on it. At the other end of the lobby was a universal cash machine, a pay phone, and a cigarette machine. August eyed the cigarette machine lustfully until Al distracted him by speaking to the desk clerk.

He was a short, balding guy who was trying to grow a moustache.

"This is another one," Al walked over to him, speaking with a husky laugh.

"I feel pretty safe with all you cops around," he announced, nodding at August.

August nodded back. "Thanks."

"If I can get you anything, just call the desk," he said before August and Al headed to the elevator.

"There's internet access, and I requested some files be sent from headquarters. Johnson also brought over some stuff this morning."

They got off on the second floor, and August followed Al down the carpeted hallway. Al slipped her key in the lock, and they both entered the narrow hallway, bathroom on one side, closet on the other. It opened out into a spacious room. Al's room had two double beds and a bureau, nightstand, and desk. A small television sat in the corner on the floor. Al had put it aside to make room for her computer equipment.

Al pointed to the small table in the far corner. "Coffee is probably cold. Sandwiches are there, tuna and chicken. That's all they had."

"It will do. I don't have much of an appetite, and coffee, well . . ." He dropped his bag. "I'd take it through a vein just about now."

She laughed. "I know the feeling. So how was Bruce?" she

asked as August pried the lid off the disposable cup. He took a sip of the brew, made a face at the bitterness and drank it down.

"He's not so great."

"Desmond came by I assume?" She sat on the bed, watching him as he grabbed a sandwich and took a bite.

"Oh yeah, he came by. He's not going to let up."

"I'm sorry if I freaked you earlier, you know, saying what I said about . . . you shooting the wrong one."

"Of course anything is possible." He sighed.

She looked at him.

"Al, don't you think I'd know if I was living with Clay all this time instead of Bruce?"

"Stranger things have happened. They were identical."

"Bruce loves me. I know that. I'd feel it even if . . ."

"Even if what?"

"He has scars. Who wouldn't? His mother locked his psychotic brother in a cellar. He watched my brother . . ." He took a breath and put down the sandwich. "He watched a killer slowly murder my brother, asking him questions he couldn't answer then using that to torture Tommy more. Something like that . . . hell, I wasn't even there, and I can't forget it. Sometimes he's moody, but he's not a killer."

"Look, I say let Desmond go on his trip. When he finds nothing, he'll have to let this go. You believe in Bruce. For now, that's good enough for me. Doesn't mean I still don't have questions."

"I know. Thanks."

"You're heading up this thing. You're the expert. I have some ideas, but I want to know how you want to proceed."

August drained the cup. "Hell. This tastes like gasoline."

"Never promised you a rose garden, honey." She snorted.

"Right." August smiled. He and Bruce had really gotten into the art of coffee making over the years, grinding different blends and investing in top of the line equipment. This coffee was painful to drink. "I'll remember that." He perched on the chair across from the bed. "You don't make coffee or do windows."

She laughed.

"I'm glad you requested the old files," August said, sobering. "That's exactly what I was going to suggest." Mr. and Mrs. Curby had both passed away now, but August remembered going to the house with Bruce when the last boy was found. They'd run Roger's Campgrounds for a long time, and they had all the registers. "One of the names on the registers, when Tommy was killed, was Bruce Monkton. It was like the killer was making a sick joke."

"The killer, the one Bruce says his brother lured here specially to kill Tommy? Bruce said in his statement that Clay murdered him and buried him under that shack out in the woods, right?"

"Right, then he burned it down."

She nodded. "But you don't believe Clay killed this guy, do you?"

"No."

"If the body had been buried under the house, even if it was burned, maybe there would be teeth, but if the body was totally burned up, it would be difficult. There might be pieces of bone. The site was searched, right?"

"Yes. They found nothing, but I want to go out there again, poke around."

"Good idea."

"I want some people assigned to track down others who were staying at the campsite at the same time as the guy who signed his name Bruce Monkton. Maybe some people remember him."

"Worth a try."

"I'm going to go by and see Dennis Jameson's parents,

and Peter Ludlow, Penny Ludlow's brother. He and Dennis were friends."

"I think we can get Desmond's boys working on that list of campers from a few years back."

"Well, you call him," August said, picking up his bag.

Al handed him his key.

"I don't really want to deal with him right now."

She nodded. "I hear you. Call me when you finish up with the witnesses. We'll take a ride out to what's left of that shack near Blood Pond. You know," she said at the door just before August left the room, "ever think there's a certain irony in the name of that pond?"

"Yeah."

"Maybe they should call it something else."

"Maybe."

"I haven't heard anything back from the locals about the diving expedition. My hunch is they won't find the body in there."

Bruce watched helplessly as Desmond and two of his officers searched the hotel room, took out his clothes, and went through the drawers.

Desmond took out the little bag filled with various toys he and August sometimes used during sex. He'd brought them all, given that this was supposed to be their little weekend alone together. Desmond of course intended to make a big show of everything as his two subordinates paused to watch.

"So, handcuffs . . ." He held them up. "Thinking of joining the force, Bruce?" He raised an eyebrow. "Cock ring?" He dangled a leather strap in the air, turning around to show it to his men.

They both stood there hiding their laughter behind their

hands.

Bruce's blood was beginning to boil.

"Clamps." He threw them on the bed. "Lube, um, what's this flavor? Chocolate sin, I bet."And these . . ." He yanked out two large dildos. With one in each hand, he waved them around. "A real cock doesn't do it for you, Bruce?"

"Are you finished?" Bruce asked between clenched teeth.

"Looks like the candy store is closed." He dumped the bag upside down. "You're a really perverted guy, aren't you, Bruce? Like to handcuff your victims before slicing off their heads?"

"Fuck you, and it's amazing you know what all those things are used for, you closeted fag."

The two officers froze, staring at Desmond. Desmond reached out with one hand and slammed Bruce into the wall. "What did you call me?"

Bruce struggled for air, beating his fists against the wall. Suddenly, Desmond released him, and Bruce slid to his knees, clutching his throat.

"Watch your mouth," he threatened, backing away. "Let's go, boys. This little cocksucker is smarter than I thought. He's buried the weapon somewhere." He looked at Bruce. "I'm watching you. And when the time comes, Bruce, you're mine."

The three cops walked out of the room, leaving the door wide open. Bruce struggled to his feet and regarded the mess. His clothes and belongings were tossed everywhere from the bed to the floor. Bruce doubled up his fist and hit the wall. Desmond Johnson was insane, obsessed with nailing him for something just because he wanted August.

But you're evil. Just because one of us is gone and buried doesn't mean the insanity will stop. You will never be worthy of a stud like August. This is never going away.

"No," Bruce cried out, placing his hands over his ears. "Go away. Go away."

As soon as he walked in, August could feel the sadness that had fallen over the house. There was a black wreath on the door, and Dennis Jameson's photograph sat prominently on the living room coffee table.

It took a few minutes until he could work himself into an actual interview. Then he had to wait for Mrs. Jameson to come downstairs.

"Can we get you something, Detective?" Mathew Jameson asked as he sat down on the sofa beside his wife, his hand tightly covering hers.

"No, thank you," August said, his gaze on the picture of the good-looking dark-haired boy in his basketball uniform. "I know I can say how sorry I am, but it really doesn't help, does it?"

"No," Mathew Jameson replied, "but I appreciate the sentiment." His wife had her head down, and she held a twisted tissue in her hand.

"I don't want to take too much of your time. I'm sure Chief Johnson has been by."

"Yes, he's been wonderful," Dennis's father replied.

"I just wanted to ask you if you noticed anything different about Dennis these last few weeks. Did his routine change, did he seem moody, withdrawn in any way?"

"No. Nothing. He was the same boy." Tears filled the father's eyes. "His room was still messy. My wife and I used to get on his case for . . . Excuse me," he said, getting up. "I need a minute."

"Of course," August said.

A few minutes later, he returned. "Please, I'm ready now." He sat back down and took his wife's hand again. "You let me know, okay?" He nodded.

"Did your son mention that he'd met anyone new?"

The man shook his head. "No."

"The last game he played on Wednesday was where?"

"Lancaster."

August wrote that down. Lancaster was less than ten miles away. "Did they win?" He tried to smile.

Mathew Jameson smiled back a little. "Yes, they won."

"Who accompanied the team when they went to play in Lancaster?" August asked.

"Volunteers. Coach Richardson, of course. Everyone looks out for everyone here. We're never short of parents who offer to ride the bus."

Coach Richardson was still at the high school? He'd been coach when August was at Whitefield.

Mrs. Jameson was crying.

He asked a few more short questions and decided it was time to leave. Before he left, August touched Mrs. Jameson's shoulder. "I'm going to find who did this, I promise you."

She raised her head then reached out and grabbed his hand. She gripped it so hard he winced. "Find that bastard, Detective. I beg you. Find him."

He nodded, and she released his hand.

Her husband led him to the door. "Detective, is it true your brother was . . ."

August met his gaze. "Yes. Twelve years ago now, so I know your pain."

"Thank you." He took his hand. "If I can tell you anything else that will help you find who did this, please call me."

"I will. I'll see you soon."

August sat outside the house for a long time just staring at it. A few days ago, it had been a different place for the people inside. He sighed and started the engine. He checked out the address for the Ludlow family and then drove on.

He had spent longer at the Jamesons than he'd intended. It was after three. Hopefully, Penny's brother would be home from school.

The Ludlow house was more modest than the Jameson's, and it was obvious from the state of the yard and the loose porch rail that the family either didn't have the time or the resources to do much house maintenance.

He parked the car and got out, glancing around the neighborhood. A teenager zipped past him on a skateboard, an elderly woman across the street was taking her clothes off the line as the clouds darkened above.

There was an old beat-up Ford in the driveway, possibly belonging to Peter, and a small yappy dog ran out to protest his arrival as he walked up the path.

The door opened before he got to the porch. A young man stood there, blond, dressed in his basketball shorts. "Skippy, come here," he snapped. "Shut up now." He looked curiously at August, who took out his badge.

"Detective Greystone. You Peter Ludlow?"

He nodded, holding onto his dog who'd stopped barking.

"Can we talk?"

"Sure. I guess. Mom," he called out.

A plump woman in a housedress came to the door, one curler on top of her dyed blonde hair. When she saw August, she patted her hair and pulled down her dress. "Well, hello. You're certainly a lot better looking than Bob."

"So, the police have come by then?"

Peter looked embarrassed as his mother pulled August inside.

"Bob came by earlier, asking me a lot of questions, but I don't know nothing, and Peter, of course, was at school."

"Did the Whitefield police go to the school today?" August asked Peter.

"No." He shook his head.

"Come on into the living room," Mrs. Ludlow said, motioning. "Don't mind the mess. I've just baked some carrot cake. I'll get some."

"No," August said, stepping over all the shoes in the hallway. The living room wasn't fancy, but there was a lot of room, and the television was a huge flat screen that filled most of the room. A tape of the Oprah show was on, and she was talking about one of her latest reads. "I just ate, thanks."

She pointed to the television, picking up the remote and switching it off. "I won that set playing bingo."

August nodded. "That's nice."

"Did you want to talk to Penny, too? She's been grounded, but she can come out of her room for you, of course, Detective." She smiled.

"No, it's alright. I came to talk to your son."

"Peter," she squawked, "get in here." She took a seat across from the sofa. "You did meet my husband, I believe, up at Blood Pond?"

"Yes, he came to get Penny that night."

"That girl is always getting herself into trouble." She leaned forward. "She gets her looks from me. And I say that good looks are a curse. You'd certainly know all about that, Detective. You remind me of some kind of a movie star . . . Rock maybe, or Cary. Definitely Cary."

August laughed a little uncomfortably.

Mrs. Ludlow screamed again for Peter, and he walked into the living room. "I'm here," he grumbled.

"Now, you answer the nice detective." She gave him a push forward.

"Ah, do you mind if I speak to Peter alone?" August asked. "Sometimes it's better."

She got up from the chair. "Of course. Police procedure I imagine. I watch those CSI shows."

"Yes, well, you'd know then," he said.

After she'd left the room, August asked Peter to sit down. He sat in the chair nearest the sofa. "I'm sorry about your friend."

"Thanks," he replied.

"Tell me about Dennis. What was he like?"

"He was cool, funny, a hell of a good basketball player. We both like video games and hanging out, you know?"

August nodded. "Did he have any problems that he was dealing with?"

"Not that I know of. He had great parents. I used to love staying there, not like here."

"Did he mention anything to you the week before this happened, talk about a new friend, or . . . someone harassing him?"

Peter shook his head.

"Tell me about the night he disappeared. When was the last time you saw him?"

"At the game. We talked a bit in town after he got off the bus then we went our separate ways."

"He walked home. Where did the bus stop?"

"In front of the diner."

That was about a five-minute walk from his house, no more.

"When you said goodbye, was there anyone left around?"

"No. I didn't notice anyone. Town gets pretty dead around eleven."

August asked him for a few more details and felt his phone vibrating in his pocket. He thanked Peter and stood. "That's all for now. Excuse me." He walked into the hallway and answered his phone.

"August, it's Al. I got Desmond's men on a research expedition, all the files came in, and the captain wants a report tonight. Anything?"

"Loose details."

"Diving expedition came up with nothing. The pond was clean."

"No weapon?"

"Nothing."

"I'll be there in about a half hour. Still want to go out to Blood Pond?"

"Yep. And August, Bruce showed up here. He's pretty upset."

"What happened?"

"Desmond went a little nuts searching the room. Bruce insisted on seeing you, and he was upset when I said you were gone. Shall I tell him you're on your way?"

"Shit. Yes. I'll be there soon." August checked his missed calls. There were four from Bruce. He had turned his phone to vibrate when he was at the Jamesons.

Peter's mother stood in front of him now. August put his phone back into his pocket. "Do you need anything else?"

"No." He held out his hand. "Thank you." He looked at Peter. "I may have a few more questions later on for you and Penny."

"My children are yours." She kept hold of his hand.

He eased it out of her grasp. "Good day." He nodded. In the car, he dialed Bruce's cell phone.

"August?"

"What happened?"

"That fucking cop. He took all my stuff out, made a mockery of me, threw my things all over the room. He . . . August, I'm scared."

"Bruce, I know it seemed overdone, but he's only doing his job." Damn it, he didn't have time for this now.

"Doing his job? Are you kidding me? You are siding with him now?"

"No, I'm not siding with anyone. Now that he's made an idiot out of himself and found nothing, he'll stop."

"He won't stop. He's said as much. He's out to get me."

"Oh, Bruce, you're being a little paranoid."

"No, I'm not fucking being paranoid. He is out to get me, and he's not going to stop until he does. He wants you. It's all about you."

"Okay, that's it. I can't listen to any of this. We'll talk about it later." He closed the connection.

He's not going to believe you. Anything you say, he'll think you're paranoid, jealous, possessive.

It was true, and Desmond Johnson knew it. He was laughing at him, just waiting to drive a wedge between August and Bruce. Bruce sank down on the bed. "Oh, Tommy, the little crush I had on you was nothing compared to what I feel for your big brother. I wonder what you'd say if you knew."

The door opened suddenly, and Bruce jumped up off the bed, his heart rate returning to normal when he saw August. He ran to him, wrapped his arms around him, held him for a moment.

August closed the door and released him. He looked down into his eyes. "Are you alright?"

"I am now that you're here. You're not leaving again, are you?"

"I'm sorry, I have to. I promised Al we'd go out to the woods near Blood Pond."

"Woods? Why? You mean to where the cabin was?"

"That's the place." August rubbed his eyes.

"Don't."

"What do you mean, don't?"

"Don't go out there, August." He walked across the room. "You won't find anything. Clay burned the place to the ground, and that maniac along with it."

"That's what he told you."

"I knew Clay better than anyone. He was in my head, August. I would have known if he was lying."

"Because you and Clay are like one. You told me that once. You really believe you can never shake off that evil stench of his."

"I am who I am, but I'm no murderer, August. I didn't put that head in Blood Pond."

He was shaking when August came over and turned him around. "I never said that. I . . ." He shook his head. "I know that."

"Do you? Even when Desmond Johnson is going to do everything he can to convince you otherwise?"

"He's wrong. Listen . . ." August sat down with him on the bed. "I have a lot of questions, a lot of things about these murders I don't understand, but I am certain of one thing. You are not a murderer."

Bruce held onto August tightly. "Stay with me," he whispered, "lie here beside me, hold me, August, make love to me."

August gently pulled away. "I can't right now. I must go. Al is waiting. Stay here, okay? I'll talk to Des, get him to back off a little."

Bruce nodded as August stood. "Try to get some sleep. You look tired."

"I don't know if I can leave here, go back to work. I'll have to call the office and . . ."

"Let me handle it," August said. "I'll make sure you get back to work."

Bruce watched August as he walked to the door. When the door closed behind him, he closed his eyes.

You're scared, aren't you? You have good reason.

CHAPTER ELEVEN

Al sat back in the passenger seat, her eyes closed as August drove back to Blood Pond. "Must have been nice growing up here," she said.

"Sometimes, but it could be boring as hell. When I turned seventeen, I wanted out of here. I was happy to join the academy, leave this place."

"Cruise men." She laughed.

"Of course, the hormones were raging."

"I grew up in Chicago, the rat race. I would have loved it here. Everyone knows everyone. That's why these murders are so shocking. Three now, including Tommy, same pattern, all around the same age, good-looking young boys. How many were there throughout the state in all?"

"Six outside of Blood Pond, starting about twenty years back. Never found the killer, the victims all around fifteen, sixteen, beheaded. Sometimes the body was found, mutilated, sexually violated, sometimes they never found the body at all."

"But none outside Blood Pond since Washington Jones three years after your brother was killed."

"No."

"Why does the killer keep coming back to Blood Pond, if it is the same one?"

"It's the same one."

"Then the burning down of that shack was just a cover-up."

August pulled the car up to the side of the road suddenly.

"Bruce says he'd know if Clay lied, but I think Bruce some-times couldn't tell where he began, and Clay ended. We have to walk from here. There's a path through the woods."

Al began to follow him into the woods. The ground was muddy after the rain, and their feet sank into the ground.

"Want me to carry your kit?" August asked as he searched the ground for the path.

"I'm fine."

"Path is overgrown, but I know it's here somewhere." August prodded the ground with his boot. "It's over there." He pointed. "Come on."

The woods got thicker as they went, blocking out the sun. "I don't like this," Al called out.

August kept walking. "Clearing is up ahead."

"Who owned the place?"

"There was no deed for it. The land belonged to the county. It was probably just a squatter place. I used to come out here as a kid and play around here."

"Morbid," she called out, hurrying to catch up.

"There it is," August said, pushing some brush aside to walk into the clearing.

Alice was breathing hard. "Or what's left of it."

"You're out of shape," he accused.

"I am. Okay, let's go."

They walked across the overgrown field to where the structure once stood. There were woods all around. Only the sounds of birds overhead and the rustling of the grass in-vaded their ears.

They both picked through some of the rubble, mostly charred wood and nails. "Nothing that looks like human remains here," she said, "but I'll bag a few things."

As she went about doing that, August stood still, his nos-trils breathing in the humid air. A shiver ran along his spine. He thought of Tommy, and this being the last place he saw before the end. He could have screamed his lungs out, and no one would have heard him out here.

When they heard a sound like someone crunching leaves and branches underfoot, August drew his gun. Al did the same, both perfectly still.

Desmond walked into the field. "Don't shoot," he called out, his hands in the air. He was smiling as he came toward them.

Al and August holstered their weapons.

"What in fuck are you doing out here?" August demanded.

"You don't seem happy to see me." He glanced over at Al. "Find anything?"

"Don't know yet," she replied.

"Tried to call you. No signal out here," Desmond said.

"What is it?"

"Seems like Bruce told a little lie when I asked him where he spent his evenings this last week."

August narrowed his eyes. "He went to a basketball game in Lancaster."

"The one on Wednesday night?" He nodded.

"So?"

"He said he spent all his nights at the hotel."

"So, he went to a game. He'd just finished a three-day conference; he was probably bored. He likes basketball."

"Why'd he lie?"

"I have no idea. Ask him yourself."

"He goes to Jameson's game, and then Jameson goes missing that night. Don't you think that's curious, August?"

"Look, what in fuck you want from me? I'll talk to him. And we need to talk about his job. He needs to go back to his office, so if you have reason to keep him in town, I'll sign a paper saying that I'm responsible if he ends up in Mexico, okay?"

"Suit yourself. I'm just doing my job." He reached out and placed a hand on August's shoulder. "You'd do the same if it was you, wouldn't you?"

August shrugged his hand off. "Bruce did not kill that boy."

"Love is blind; lust is blinder. I must admit," Desmond said, lowering his voice as he came to stand beside August, "he's a nice little package, young, blond, great body, but August really . . . Is it worth it to put everything on the line for a piece of ass?"

August glanced at him. He told himself not to lose his temper. "I love him, Desmond. We love each other. We're not hiding in any closet. We're a couple; something you wouldn't know anything about."

"I'd do anything for you, August." He met his gaze. "I made mistakes but not this time. This time I'll do it right, and in the end, you'll see everything clear as day."

August narrowed his eyes. He was about to ask him to explain what he meant, but Al came walking over, wiping the dirt from her knees.

"Okay, I got what I want, but I doubt it will produce anything."

"Because there's nothing to produce," August said.

Desmond nodded. "He's right. No killer ever died here. He's still out there."

The three of them walked side by side through the field. "Time to call it a day," August said. "I'm going back to the hotel, call the captain, and get some sleep."

Desmond stopped before getting in his car. "Got my men working on hunting down former campers that were at Roger's at the time of Tommy's murder. Not sure it will produce much though," he said to August.

"Worth a try," August said. "Keep me posted. And, Des," He sighed as Al got into the car. "Try to give me a break where Bruce is concerned."

He nodded and walked to his cruiser.

When they reached the hotel, August turned back to Al before walking into his hotel room. "Tomorrow, I'll go and have a talk with the coach at the high school, see if he can tell me anything."

"Good idea. I'll send this stuff away for testing. Should have the results in twenty-four hours or so."

"Goodnight, Alice," he said.

"August..." She looked at him. "Ask Bruce about the basketball game." He nodded.

Bruce was sitting on the bed watching some comedy show when August walked in. He was happy to see him and hungry. It was almost eight o'clock.

"Hi," he said, "I waited with supper. Want to go out to eat? Diner is open until ten."

"Can we send out?" August put away his gun and stripped off his shirt. "I'm beat."

"Sure. I'll call over there. What do you want?"

"Whatever," he called from the bathroom.

Bruce heard the shower turn on. He picked up the phone and ordered pizza and fries.

When August came out, a towel around his waist, Bruce desperately wanted to rip it away. He wasn't sure what was more pressing, his hunger for food or his hunger for August's cock.

"Food coming?"

"Um..." August looked tired, and Bruce wasn't sure if he'd be in the mood. "I need you," he said.

August glanced at him. "I need you, too." He smiled, but he didn't touch him. "How long before the food gets here? I'm starving."

"They said thirty minutes."

August opened his suitcase and took out a pair of sweat-pants. Bruce watched him dry off, following the lines of his hips and thighs with his gaze and dug his nails into the mattress. Their passion for each other was as intense now as it always had been. At least it was for Bruce. Sex was healing for him; it soothed him and took away the pain, the anger.

When he was away from August's body too long, he grew restless, the anxiety mounting inside him. "You're my Prozac," he said, reaching for August's hand after he slipped into the navy sweatpants.

August laughed. He crawled onto the bed and pulled him into his arms. Bruce laid his head on August's chest, and August stroked his hair. "Is that so?" he whispered.

Bruce's hand snaked down inside August's waistband. He fondled his cock with greedy fingers until August's breath came fast and hard. "Um," he murmured, his hips rising a little. "Bruce," he groaned, "the food is coming."

"You first." He chuckled, pulling the sweatpants down over August's erection. "I love your cock. It's so big and thick, and I want you." He lowered his lips to August's shaft, licking up the length of it.

August pressed Bruce's head a little, and Bruce took him into his mouth. He took his time licking and suckling until August's cum flowed into his mouth and between his teeth, and he heard his grunt of satisfaction.

Bruce pressed his cheek to August's groin and felt his fingers on his hair again. "Thanks, baby," August said. "After we eat, you will fuck me, won't you?"

"If I have the strength," August told him.

They lay there together quietly, just enjoying that closeness until a rap sounded on the door. "That's the food." Bruce jumped off the bed and went to the door, giving the guy a big tip because neither had any change. He brought the food back to bed.

They both ate heartily, and Bruce opened the bar and found two small bottles of red wine. They drank it out of plastic glasses then Bruce cleared everything off the bed and crawled on top of August.

"Fuck me." He kissed him hard on the mouth.

August's tongue mingled sweetly with his, and he felt August's passion rise. "Please, baby. I need you now."

It didn't matter that it wasn't the most energetic coupling they'd ever had, but it was slow and deep, and oh so satisfying. Bruce had needed to feel August inside of him, to reassure him that despite everything, it was going to be alright.

They didn't talk. August fell asleep with his groin nestled against Bruce's backside and his arm secured around his waist.

Enjoy it while you can, Bruce.

He was walking in the open field, a small shack in the clearing. Clay stood at the door. He waved at him and smiled as he motioned with his hand. "Come on, come in. Everyone is here now."

Bruce shook his head.

August is here. He's a beautiful man.

"No." Bruce began to run toward the cabin. "No, don't you touch him. Don't touch him, please."

Only his head. We'll give you his head, boy.

Bruce couldn't breathe. He felt around in the darkness, his hands sliding over the wall. "Please," he pleaded, sobbing, "take me. Not August, not him. Not August."

Suddenly he looked down, and there, rolling across the floor, was the head. Two blue eyes looked up at him, dead. "Dead. Dead. No! August!"

He was fighting hard, screaming. He couldn't seem to get his breath.

"Bruce! Bruce, for Christ's sake, stop it. It's me. It's August; you're safe." Strong arms were pinning him down.

Bruce's eyes snapped open. He looked up into August's face. They'd fallen asleep with the lamp on. He quieted, reached up to touch his cheek. "August?"

"Yes, baby, it's me." He kissed his forehead. "You had a bad dream?"

Bruce sat up in the bed. "There were three."

"Three what?" August asked sleepily, rubbing his eyes.

"Three of them, including Clay. Clay said come in . . . and there were two more, and they . . ." He took a breath. "They cut off . . . your head."

August's eyes widened a little.

Bruce lowered his face to his shoulder and sobbed.

It took a long time for August to calm Bruce down. He didn't want to sleep, and he didn't want August to sleep either. "No one is going to cut off my head, Bruce." He had to admit he was becoming a little impatient and irritable. He was exhausted, and the clock said it was two fifteen in the morning.

"It was so real," Bruce said.

"But it wasn't real," August told him, trying to hold on to his temper. "It was just a dream. Come back to bed."

"I can't. You go ahead."

August lay there watching Bruce as he stood looking out the window into the deep night. He looked so alone. Even after all this time, Bruce was still somewhat of a mystery, a tragic loner whose life should have never involved all that tragedy. "Bruce, why didn't you tell Desmond about the basketball game?"

He turned and looked at him, seeming surprised at the question. "Why do you think? Isn't it obvious? I knew he'd make a big deal out of it. Now, you're going to do that, too, aren't you?"

"No, I just don't think it was a good idea to lie to the police, that's all."

"I went, I watched the game, I came home. Woman in the diner mentioned it to me when I went to eat some supper. You know I like basketball." August nodded.

"He's out to get me. Why would I give him more ammunition?"

"Desmond is not out to get you."

"Yes, he is. He's a bastard. Do you know that he held up all those sex toys I brought with me to the hotel and flashed them around to his men, making comments, laughing?"

August narrowed his eyes. "He had no right to do that. He can be a little weird sometimes I admit but — "

"A little weird? He's jealous. He hates me because he wants to be with you."

"That's not it. He's a cop in a small town who would have liked to work homicide in Manchester. This is a big thing for him, and he's getting a little carried away."

"If he wanted to be a city cop so bad, why didn't he just apply to work in the city? He could have been close to you." Bruce sneered. "He'd be in heaven. What's he doing here playing chief of police then?"

August had wondered that himself. "I don't know. I suppose he had a better chance for advancement here, a quieter life."

"He doesn't want a quieter life. You just finished telling me that he had big ambitions. So, which is it?"

"Bruce," August said with a sigh, "right now, I really don't care to speculate on why Desmond decided to work in Whitefield. Truly, I don't know, and I don't really care, okay? Now, I'm tired. Can we just get some sleep?"

"I'm sorry," Bruce replied. "I know you're tired. Go ahead. I'll just sit here and watch the sun come up."

"Do what you want," August grumbled, rolled over in bed, and dragged the covers up over his head. He dropped off to sleep almost immediately.

Bruce stretched out in one of the chairs and stared at the ceiling. *Be careful. I tried to warn you.*

He ran his thumb over his phone, muted the volume, and turned it on. The screen announced that he had seven new messages. The first emails had arrived in his box last night. He didn't know whether to tell August or not. He'd been upset about Desmond ransacking his room earlier then, just before August had arrived last night, his phone beeped. He was sure it was the office. He'd already notified them that he might have to take the week off. The message was sent from a mobile phone. The subject line read *Blood Pond get out.* There was nothing else. The body of the message was empty. After that, ten more messages arrived, all from the same mobile phone, number restricted, and all of them identical. Either someone was trying to warn him, or to scare him.

He checked his messages again. This time there was one from the office, but no others. He breathed a sigh of relief and turned the phone off.

Eventually, he drifted off to sleep, but there was a voice in his head, a face peering at him. *You don't know. You've forgotten. Be careful. He's here. He's close. They want you ... want to draw you back into their games. He made me this way ...*

"Bruce?" It was August speaking to him. "Want to get some breakfast?"

Bruce yawned and opened his eyes. His phone fell on the floor beside him. He nodded. "Do I have time for a shower?"

"Sure, I've got to see Al."

"Does she have to come, too?" Bruce grunted, sitting up.

August eyed him. "I wasn't going to invite her but ... Bruce, Al is a good friend of mine."

"She hates me."

"Why in hell do you think everyone hates you? You got a real complex," he muttered and left the room.

Bruce sighed. *Wasn't that the truth?*

August hated it when Bruce got bitchy, claiming the entire world was against him. Yeah, Al wasn't Bruce's biggest fan, but she certainly didn't *hate* him. In fact, she was always nice to him whenever he was around.

Al shouted to August to come in when he knocked.

She was huddled over files, sitting cross-legged on the bed. "Hey, August."

"Hey yourself. Want to get some breakfast with me and Bruce?"

"No, I ate something early this morning."

"I'm going to see my old coach today, talk to him about Dennis Jameson."

"That's right," she said with a laugh, "you went to White-field High, didn't you?"

"Yeah. It wasn't a bad school now that I look back."

"Heard from Desmond?"

"No."

"He called this morning. I'm sure there's a message on your phone. Says one of the officers found a man who was staying at the campground at the time of Tommy's murder."

"Great. I'll give him a call."

"Forensics came back."

"And?"

"As you suspected . . . nothing. If someone did burn up there, there's nothing left of them now. Funny, they didn't sweep the area back when your brother died."

"They didn't know about it. Don't forget, Bruce had left, and there was really nothing to go on at all."

She looked thoughtful.

"I'll call you later," August said. "I want to go over all the murders and match up some things."

"I hear you."

When they got to the diner, Bruce seemed edgy. He didn't eat half his breakfast and kept playing with his phone. "What's wrong?" August asked him.

Bruce shrugged and glanced around then back down at his phone.

The diner was full, and people stared over at them every once in a while and whispered to each other. They knew who Bruce and August were. The whole town knew, and it made for colorful gossip.

"Don't pay attention to them," August said. "They're small-minded and . . . well, they don't understand."

"What they don't understand is how you can share breakfast and your bed with the brother of the psychopath who chopped your brother's head off."

"Bruce!"

Bruce pushed back the chair and walked out of the diner.

August sighed, threw some money on the table, and followed him outside. When he got outside, Bruce was fiddling with his phone again. "Fuck."

"What is it? What's the matter?" August asked, taking out his sunglasses and perching them on his nose. It was cool today, but the sun was intense despite it. "What?" August insisted as Bruce reluctantly handed over his phone. August stared at it. "When did you start receiving these?" he demanded.

"Last night."

"Why in hell didn't you tell me?"

"Could be anyone here in town, couldn't it? I felt the hostility when I was inside."

"Could be," August replied, "but it might be something

more. I need your phone."

"No," he said. "August, what if the office calls?"

"Call Judy and tell her to redirect your calls to my cell. If there is anything, I'll let you know." Bruce nodded.

"Thanks for telling me. Come on, I'll drop you back to the hotel. I must get over to the high school. Try not to worry; it's probably nothing."

Ten minutes later, August handed Bruce's phone to Al and let her see the emails. "Shit," she said, looking up at him. "What's your theory?"

"Some ass in the town maybe. They all know the history."

"They think it's strange that you're with the guy whose brother killed yours?"

"Basically."

"August," she said, "can I ask you a question, something I've been wanting to ask for a long time?"

"Go ahead."

"How exactly did you and Bruce come together? You're so different."

"Loss brought us together, Bruce's connection to Tommy. He had a crush on him." He smiled. "They were best friends that summer, and then he was there when . . . when he died. I thought Bruce could help me find this guy. Instead, we found his twin who claimed to have lured a psycho here then burned him up in that shack. We just needed each other."

"And now, still?"

"Look, I know Bruce can be . . . well, different, moody, insanely jealous, but he also can be the most straightforward, loving, and generous man I've ever known. When we're together, when the demons are at bay, there's no one better. He keeps me from turning inside myself, brooding, and the passion we share, the bond . . . I just want to protect him forever. He can be like a fragile little boy."

She nodded. "You really love him."

"Oh yes," he said softly, "I do. And before all this at Blood Pond again, I really thought we'd put it behind us. He started the business, and I'm happy on the force. We have a nice house, a great life, and we have our petty arguments, but . . . now, it's like we're at square one. He's so scared, and having bad dreams, hearing voices in his head. I'm afraid he's going to need to see someone."

"It's going to be alright, August." She put her arms around him. "I'll send this off, see if we can find out whose phone it came from, okay?"

"Thanks," he said. "I'm off to the high school."

"I'll be here most of the day, and I'll have one of Desmond's men pick up the phone and send it off. I'll keep an eye on Bruce if you like."

"I'd appreciate that," he said.

It was strange being back at his old high school. It was a four-story building with a huge gym and a running track outside. There was red brick and concrete everywhere, which was so typical of schoolhouses, and of course, the flag waved proudly above the entrance.

He climbed the front steps and pressed the buzzer. They never had one when he was there. Anyone could walk into the school, but then this was Whitefield, and no one had worried about that stuff back then.

When a voice came over the intercom, he said, "Detective Greystone, Manchester police. I'm here to see Coach Hal Richardson."

The buzzer sounded, and August pulled the door open. That school smell invaded his senses, the smell of erasers, gym shoes, and photocopy toner. He walked down the corridor a little way, past the grade seven lockers, and turned the corner to the administration office.

A woman sat behind the counter and got up from her desk when he appeared. "Hello," he said, "I'm Detective Greystone."

The woman smiled. "Principal Hewitt will be with you in a moment."

Suddenly, a door opened just across the hall, and a woman, dressed in a gray tailored suit, came out to greet him. "Detective Greystone," she said, holding out her hand, "my name is Donna Hewitt. I'm the school principal."

He shook her hand. "Nice to meet you."

"Please come into my office. I've already paged Hal. He's just getting someone to take over his class, and he'll be right here. Won't you sit down?"

"Thank you," August said.

"Coffee?"

"No, thank you."

Principal Hewitt sat down behind her big, mahogany desk. She was a woman in her fifties with neatly coiffed gray hair and an air of authority. "It's been tough for everyone at Whitefield, especially those in Dennis's class. We've had grief counsellors here for the students."

"Of course. What kind of a student was Dennis?"

"He was an honors student, very bright, a great basketball player."

"What about his personality? Would you describe him as an introvert, a party guy?"

"He was very quiet, polite, he had friends, but he wasn't the kind to make trouble."

"I see."

"Sorry it took me a while," a voice suddenly boomed from behind them.

August turned to see his old football coach standing there, twenty pounds heavier and with a few extra lines in his face. He stood and held out his hand. "Hello, Coach, how are you?"

"August, August Greystone, my God. A detective, eh?" He shook his hand.

August smiled.

"I thought he was going to the NBA," the coach said to Principal Hewitt.

"Yeah, right." August chuckled.

"You can use my office," the principal said with a smile. She nodded at August and left, closing the door.

"Horrible about the Jameson kid," the coach said, perching on the desk.

August sat back down in the chair. "Yes."

"Reminds me when Tommy got killed, nice kid, your brother."

"Thanks." August swallowed.

"What in hell is wrong with this world, August?"

"I don't know, sir," he said. "Wish I knew. Coach, can you tell me about Dennis, about the night of the game before he disappeared?"

"Routine game, lot of players out sick for some reason. Dennis got a lot of court time. He scored a few, too. He had potential, that kid."

"Can you tell me who the chaperones were?"

"Ah, myself," He began to count on his fingers. "Darcy French, my assistant, Dan Florence, Stan Florence's dad. He's our forward."

"These were usually the people who went on road trips?"

"Usually."

"Who was there from Whitefield?"

"Hell, practically everyone who counts, the principal, the mayor, the chief of police, the town doctor and his wife, most of the teachers, and I'd say most of the parents and the students here at Whitefield, except Dennis's mother. She didn't come out to many of the games."

"Anyone suspicious hanging around you didn't know, talking with the boys?"

"No one I noticed. Wish I could tell you more. Damn, this shouldn't have happened. The whole town is petrified. We thought this was all over when you shot Clay Monkton. People are beginning to think Bruce had more to do with it." He stopped. "I know he's your friend."

August stood. "My lover. And Bruce did not kill Dennis Jameson." He met the coach's gaze.

"Just saying." He looked down at the carpet.

"Thanks for your time." He walked out into the hallway, and his phone rang. He was at the front door when the principal appeared. He held up his hand and answered the phone.

"Hey, it's me," Alice said into the receiver. "Any luck?"

"Not much. I need to truck up on to the other school in Lancaster."

"Did you get Desmond's message?"

"No, is it about the guy who was camping at Roger's?"

"Yeah."

"I haven't listened to it yet."

"The man will be here tomorrow. Desmond says you're welcome to go to the station and question him."

He was welcome? "Since when is Desmond in charge of this case?"

"Have no idea."

"Great. I'll stop by and find out the details before I drive up to Lancaster. Any news on Bruce's phone?"

"Still waiting on that. Bruce has been in his room all day. I went to check on him, and he told me he was tired. Didn't want to be bothered, I think. Desmond asked me if Bruce was still here. Wants me to keep an eye on him, not the same motive as yours I'm afraid."

"Right, okay, call me if you need me." He hung up.

He was back there in that cold barn. His twin was bleeding and so was he, so hurt, cold, so filled with misery and disbelief, he almost didn't call August to rescue him. They'd talked—his brother rambled mostly—and it was only now that the conversation came back to him, for some reason, and it was compelling.

Bruce frantically searched his memory, trying to recall the exact words his brother had spoken. "You were lucky really. He didn't get to you. He wanted to. He got to them."

"Them?"

"He let them play before the end. I never wanted to hurt them. You got to believe me. He expected loyalty. He was really disappointed in you."

"Shut up, I don't want to hear about that animal you lured here."

"I didn't really lure him, Bruce. He wanted to come. He was waiting to come. I was never in control. It's not over. You think just because your big hero, August, will come to rescue you, it's over. It will never be over until he says. There are too many . . . too many and they hide him."

Bruce jumped up from the chair. He paced, then glanced out the window. The wind blew through the trees, and he shuddered as they seemed to whisper, *there are too many . . . too many, and they hide him.*

August walked into the Whitefield Police Station, intending to have no more than a brief meeting with Desmond. When he arrived, however, Desmond wasn't there.

"He's out, sweetie," the dispatcher said, grinning at him. "You can wait. Want something? Coffee, juice, me?"

"No, thanks." August gave her a curious look. "I can

59

come back."

"He just stepped out, won't be long. Want me to call him?"

"No, I—"

"August, there you are," Desmond boomed, bursting through the front door. "I've been waiting on you. You don't answer my messages anymore or what?"

"I've been busy."

"Told you he was coming," the woman with the phone at her ear announced.

"Come to my office; we need to talk," Desmond invited.

August followed him in. "Desmond, no more talk about Bruce, okay?"

He put up his hands. "No problem. I have good news. A man by the name of Marvin Greenly will be here tomorrow. He was camping here when Tommy was killed. He says he remembers someone with a tattoo on his forearm."

"That's good. What time is the interview?"

"Nine, if you can drag yourself away from that sweet hot thing you got in your bed."

"Right." August decided to ignore it. "Anything other than that to report?"

"Nope, heard about the phone thing. I bet it's just some-one here in town who doesn't like your boyfriend."

"Yes," August said, looking at him, "like you?"

He laughed. "No time to terrorize twinks."

"Right. I'll be here at nine."

"August . . ." Desmond came around and blocked his way. "You and I . . . we—"

"There is no you and I, Des."

"What in hell you got in common with that nutcase?" He laughed a little, but the laugh was angry.

"You want to move out of my way, please?"

Desmond moved.

"See you tomorrow," August told him, "and, Desmond, try not to forget who's in charge of this investigation, okay?"

His mouth twisted a little. "Right."

Pure fucking insanity.

August started the motor then pulled to the side as his phone rang. He saw that it was Al. "What's up?"

"Got the news back on Bruce's phone. The caller's phone is registered to a Cynthia Price. And listen to this. She's a prison guard up in the penitentiary for women. She reported her phone missing a few days ago."

"Shit," August muttered, pulling away from the curb. "That's where Bruce's mother is."

CHAPTER TWELVE

When August told Bruce, "The messages are from your mother," Bruce almost fell over.

"No," he said. "That's impossible."

"She stole a guard's cell phone."

"Why in hell would my mother . . ."

"She's trying to warn you about something."

"What?"

August threw up his hands. "If I knew that, I wouldn't be asking you. Think!"

"I have no fucking idea. My mother hates me."

"She doesn't hate you. And why do I think you know more about this than you're telling me?"

"Maybe you've been hanging around with your friend Desmond too long," he accused, his voice rising in volume with each word.

"Bruce. Goddamn it."

He sighed. "I've got to take a walk."

An hour later, August was sitting at the bar and grill with Alice. "He'll come around," she said. "He was probably surprised, that's all. What do you make of all this?"

August slugged back his beer and shook his head. "I don't know. The only way is for me to go up to the prison and talk to her, take Bruce with me."

"Will he go?"

"He will if I say so."

"Who will if you say so?" a voice boomed.

Al and August glanced up to see Desmond slip into a chair at their table. He signaled the waitress. "Beer all around," he called out.

"What are you guys doing in here crying in your beer?" he asked with a grin.

The waitress came over with the glasses and set them down on the table.

"Thank you, honey," Des said, placing a bill on her tray. "Keep the change," he added with a wink.

August wanted to roll his eyes. He always hated when Desmond put on the straight act. He was damn good at it.

"No one is crying," Al said. "We're talking about Bruce's phone."

"I never did trust Evelyn Monkton. Imagine locking your kid in the cellar just because he was mentally retarded." Des picked up his beer glass.

"Clay wasn't mentally retarded," August argued. "He was mentally disturbed."

"Whatever. She harbored him, hid him in a basement. That can't be good for anybody," he said, taking a swig of his ale.

August sighed. "I admit she's eccentric."

"What do you think she's warning Bruce about?" Al asked.

"She's not warning him about anything," Desmond scoffed. "She's tipping him off. She's probably the one who talks in his head now, gives him orders to kill."

August didn't think; he just reacted. He jumped to his feet and reached across the table, grabbing Desmond by the shirt.

"Whoa." Desmond tried to push August's hands off. "What in fuck is your problem?"

"You, you're my problem. Shut your fucking mouth. This

is a police investigation. You don't go speculating about guilt in a Goddamned bar. Now, I've given you free rein so far, but don't forget who's in charge. You got it?"

Desmond nodded. "Sure. Fuck. Relax, okay?"

August released him and sat back in his seat.

Desmond cleared his throat and straightened his shirt. Al smiled faintly. Any guy with common sense would have left then, but Desmond just smiled and drank down his beer.

Silence ensued as the three of them sat there. August was the first to stand up. "I'm going back to the hotel. I'll be there tomorrow." He looked at Desmond.

"Don't start until I get there."

"Guess I'll fly too," Al said, getting up as well. She followed August out of the bar.

August was spitting fire when he got outside. Al placed a hand on his arm. "You okay? You really lost it in there."

"Too bad I never realized what a dumb fuck he was before."

"Never mind him. Remind me not to piss you off." She laughed and took his arm.

He smiled at her. "Don't piss me off."

When August got back to the hotel room, he was relieved to find Bruce there.

"I'm sorry, baby," Bruce said, running into his arms as soon as he closed the door. "Don't be angry with me."

"I'm not angry," August told him. "I want you come with me to see your mother."

He broke away from him. "Why?"

"Maybe she'll tell us the real reason she sent those messages."

Bruce took a breath. "What? Maybe I don't want to know."

"Sometimes, babe, the things you don't want to know are the things you must know."

Bruce seemed to relax. He smiled at him, reached up and kissed his cheek. "My, you are the philosopher tonight, handsome. Want to serenade me to bed?"

August pulled him close. "You read my mind."

Marvin Greenly, the camper they'd located, turned out to be a man in his sixties, who had been quite battered by life. He'd worked at various jobs wherever he could find them and didn't have a lot of formal education. When August arrived, Greenly was sitting in the small conference room beside the holding cell with a cup of coffee in front of him.

Desmond took him into the room and introduced August. "This is Detective Greystone," he said, "a big city detective. He's going to ask you a few questions."

August glanced at Desmond. "Do you mind giving us a minute alone?" He didn't much care for Desmond's attitude. Let's intimidate the guy before we get two words out of him.

Sure, I'll be right outside if you should need me, sir."

It was a slur. August thought it best to ignore him. He had no idea why Desmond was being such an asshole, but his behavior was getting on August's last nerve.

"They treating you alright, Marvin?" August asked. "You don't mind if I call you Marvin, do you?"

"No, not at all, sir."

"Please," August said, doing up his jacket to conceal his weapon as he took a seat across from him, "call me August. My father used to call me Gus."

He chuckled. "You look more like an August to me if you don't mind me saying it."

August smiled. "No, that's fine. So, if there's anything you need, Marvin, while you're here, I'll give you my number, and you can call me, okay?"

"They been a treating me real nice, sir . . . I mean . . . August. Nice hotel and meals at the diner. Couldn't ask for more than that."

"Good. So, Marvin, tell me about the time you were staying out at Roger's Campground. What were you doing out there? On vacation?"

"Nope. I was working in the woods, clearing some brush for the town. My brother-in-law worked for the municipality, and they were looking for people, so I came on down."

"Were you alone?"

"Yep, never did find me a proper wife, not easy to live with I guess." He grinned. "I like the bach life."

August smiled. "So, tell me about this guy, the one with the tattoo. What made him stand out?"

"When that cop called me and asked me about people staying at the campground here at that time, I didn't know what to tell him at first. I had to really think about it. It was busy, filled with people, all kinds of people from everywhere. Then, after I hung up, I got to thinking about that fellow with the tattoo on his arm, and I called that officer back. I spoke to him just once. He wasn't what'd you call a real social fellow, stuck to himself, had a tent set up back in the trees. Didn't come out and talk to people around the campfires at night."

"Tell me about the time you spoke with him."

"We met in the bathroom, and he asked me if I had a light. I gave him some spare matches I had. It was then I noticed the dragon on his forearm. I told him I liked it. He didn't say much, took the matches and left."

"Can you describe him?"

"Not a big fellow that I remember, fair-haired, not heavy, but muscles, well put together. Had a beard I think."

"What was he wearing?"

Pair of jeans, light-colored t-shirt. Running shoes."

"Could you say how old he was?"

"Ah, I'd say about thirty-five, going on forty."

"Did he say his name?"

"Monkton said his name was Monkton. Never did get a first name though. Like I said, he wasn't too friendly like."

August nodded. That corresponded with what he'd found on the register. The guy had signed his name Bruce Monkton . . . some kind of a sick joke maybe.

"Did you ever see him with anyone while you were there? Anyone come onto the campgrounds, into his tent?"

"Nope, not that I saw. Like I said, he stuck to himself."

"Did he arrive before you, or after?"

"He was there when I arrived. I don't remember the exact date."

"It's alright. We have that on file. And were you still there when he left?"

"Yep. One day I woke up around seven in the morning and his tent was gone."

"How many days after you arrived?"

"I'd say two, no more."

August nodded and stood. He held out his hand.

"Thank you, Marvin, you've been very helpful."

"I hope you catch this crazy," he said.

"So do I," August replied.

That afternoon, August, Desmond, and Alice sat in the conference room going over what they had so far when August excused himself to take a call from the captain. "There are lots of threads," Affleck told him on the phone. "We need a suspect. What's your next move?"

"Visit Evelyn Monkton in the prison," August said. "I'm also going to get the locals to interview everyone that was on that bus, and at the game the night the Jameson kid was taken."

"Good. Desmond Johnson has been in touch with me, August. He suggested you may have a blind side on this one."

"That fucking . . ." August muttered. "That's not true."

"What about where Bruce Monkton is concerned? August, I'm sorry, but he's the only suspect we got. He had opportunity, and he doesn't have a proper alibi. He was also at the game that night. Given his background and his connection with all this stuff before — "

Listen, I take full responsibility for Bruce, okay?"

"I'll give you another week, August, that's it," he said and hung up.

August came into the conference room like a cyclone. Alice and Desmond looked up from something they were reading.

"How dare you go to my captain behind my back." He glared at Desmond.

Desmond sighed.

Al's eyes widened.

"I only spoke to him about your lack of objectivity on this one, August. This is serious. You're fucking the only suspect in the case."

"Al," August said, never taking his eyes off Desmond, "can you give us a minute?"

"August, don't kill him," Alice said, then she looked at Desmond. "You don't do this, Desmond, stab your brothers in the back. It was wrong." She walked out and closed the door.

August paced a few minutes, telling himself to calm down. "Listen, Desmond, I don't want this tension between us. We must work together somehow. And, in some way, I can even understand where this is coming from, but you have to trust me when it comes to Bruce. I *know* him."

"Do you? Do you really know him?" Desmond insisted.

He got up and came around the table to stand in front of August. "I apologize. I was out of line. I shouldn't have called your superior. I shouldn't have harassed Bruce the way I did. I admit it; I'm jealous." He shrugged and sighed. "I've made so many mistakes. I realize when I see you what I could have had if only I'd had the guts."

"Desmond, I—" August began.

"No, hear me out. I see you with him, and I just go a little nuts. He's not good enough for you, August, and like it or not, he's a prime suspect, and you know it, don't you? As a cop, deep in your gut, you know it."

When August didn't answer right away, Desmond said it again, meeting his gaze. "Don't you?"

August nodded silently. He did, but somehow, he knew it wasn't true. He knew that these past few years he'd spent with Bruce weren't a lie. They *couldn't* be. "You need to trust me to do the right thing, Desmond, if the time comes when I . . ." He stopped.

"I do trust you. I trust you with my life." He lowered his voice. "I love you, August. I always have. And I'll stand by you in this no matter what happens. Forgive me?"

August nodded. "Let's put it behind us and concentrate on this case, okay?"

"It's a deal."

I need some coffee," August said.

That night, Bruce noticed how quiet August was. They had eaten at the diner then gone back to the hotel. Last night, August had made love to him, sweet, beautiful love, and he'd felt as if nothing could ever hurt him. Tonight, he felt alone, felt as if there was a brick wall between them. "Where are you?" he asked him suddenly, coming up behind August in the chair and wrapping his arms around his neck.

August turned and smiled at him. "Here, with you."

"Are you? Are we drifting apart?"

"No," August said, pulling away. He got out of the chair. "I'm just preoccupied, that's all. Greenly said the guy at the campground remembers a man with a tattoo saying his name was Bruce Monkton."

"Why would he have used my name? I never understood that."

"I don't know. Will you come with me to see your mother tomorrow?"

"Do I have a choice?" The last person he wanted to see was Evelyn.

"Please."

"August, if you make love to me the way you did last night, I'll go anywhere with you and see anyone."

August smiled back and opened his arms. "You drive a hard bargain, baby." He chuckled, tickling him.

"But . . . well . . . okay."

Bruce took his hand and pulled him to the bed. "Poor baby," Bruce teased, undoing his pants. "I torture you so."

August closed his eyes and let the sensation of Bruce's movements with his tongue carry him away.

"I love you, August," Bruce whispered.

"I know," he said, touching Bruce's silky blond hair. *Could I bear it if it was true? Is Desmond right, that my love for you blinds me to the fact that you could be a coldblooded killer? God, will the doubt ever end . . . will he . . .*

His hips lifted off the mattress, and his body shuddered with release. He closed his eyes as his tongue moved over his lips. Bruce snuggled up close to him. August pulled him even closer.

"I'm so afraid to lose you," Bruce said against his ear.

How could he tell him that he feared the same thing?

"Don't leave me. You'll stay with me tomorrow when we go to see Evelyn, won't you? You won't leave me alone with her, will you?"

"No," August said, looking at him. "I'll be right beside you. I promise." He kissed his mouth tenderly then rolled Bruce over onto his stomach and started to kiss his shoulders and down his spine.

There were no words for how much Bruce loved this man, and his fear of being without him that somehow, he'd lose him was so intense, he could feel it in his very soul. He tried not to think about that as August made love to his body, but the voices were louder than ever, warning him of what was to come.

He wasn't sure who was talking to him. It might have even been his own buried memories reminding him that there was so much he'd forgotten. Why was Evelyn warning him, and what was she warning him of? His twin was dead; he couldn't hurt him anymore, couldn't hurt anyone anymore. That maniac who'd killed Tommy . . . Wasn't he dead too? No, he wasn't dead. Just as he feared years ago when he escaped through the woods and kept on running . . . he should have never come back here. He knew one day *he'd* get him.

The fear floated outside of him now, shadows on the walls, sounds of cars outside, someone laughing. He was caught up now in August's strong arms, his passion, as this man rose and fell inside of him. Nothing mattered at this moment except this. He cried out with pleasure and bathed in contentment in the arms of his lover.

August fell asleep soon after, but Bruce stayed awake and listened to the sound of August's heart beating strongly. Its steady rhythm filled him with hope, then he heard the voice. *You belong to me, Bruce. You can run, but you'll never hide. I'll see you soon.*

August had told him they were leaving early in the morning to head up to the prison. August's police friend, Alice, was coming with them. Bruce didn't care really. He was stressed out as it was, and her tagging along didn't make a difference. August seemed to think his mother might open up more to a woman. August didn't know his mother.

Bruce waited impatiently in the car as August spoke with Desmond outside on the front steps of the police station. Their heads were bent together as they read some words on a notepad. "I'll give you a report when I get back," August called to him as he headed to the car.

"Wonder what that's about," Bruce commented from the back seat.

Alice turned around and gave him a shrug. "Who knows with those two?"

Bruce glanced at August as he got in the car and behind the wheel. "Desmond looked pissed off."

"When is he not pissed off lately?" August grumbled as he started the engine.

Desmond stood staring at them as they drove away. Bruce turned around and looked at him through the back window, and Desmond seemed to smile.

"What now?" Alice asked August as Bruce turned back around.

"He wanted to come with us."

"Why?" Bruce blurted.

"I guess he wanted to be in on the interview. I said I'd give him a report. He's so afraid of missing something."

"Oh, and do you think you've missed something?" Bruce asked.

August looked at Bruce in the rearview mirror as he took the road out of Whitefield. "What does that mean?"

"I . . . I don't know really, nonsense, I guess. Forget it," Bruce said.

"They're busy enough there," Alice added, "questioning people, teachers at the school, and so on. You'd think he'd be more interested in supervising what his own men are doing than looking over your shoulder all the time."

"Yes, everyone is a suspect." Bruce tried to sound comical. "Even your ninety-year-old grandmother is not above suspicion."

"Funny boy." August smiled.

Alice laughed a little. "He's right, given the fact that we have so few leads."

"You alright?" August asked Bruce.

"Sure."

"You didn't eat any breakfast."

"I'm a little stressed."

"She can't hurt you."

"I know. Does she know we're coming?"

"No. Only the warden. I didn't think it was a good idea to tip her off, give her time to prepare too much."

"Is the prison far?" Alice asked.

"No, Goffstown is not far from Bedford. An hour or so and we'll be there."

"Think I'll nap. You mind?" Bruce asked.

"Go ahead," August said.

Bruce closed his eyes. Someone was smiling at him in his mind. *It won't be long now. He's waiting for you.*

Electronic cameras were everywhere, and women wore blue-gray smocks with numbers plastered on their breast pockets. August and Alice seemed at home here, walking confidently through the hallway as they followed the warden.

Women stared at them as they paused in their work de-

73

---

tail, mopping the floor or pushing around the library cart. Someone said, "Hi, honey," to August, who didn't pay any attention.

The warden stopped at another glass partition and pressed in a code. The door slid open with the sound an air compressor might make. Bruce felt the sound vibrate all the way down to his shoes.

The warden, a short, stocky woman with hair the color of straw, led them to an empty room with a long table and a couple of chairs. "She's on her way," the warden said. "The guard will remain outside the door, but I've given instructions for the door to be closed, Detective."

"Thank you," August said.

"You didn't tell her who was here to see her?" Alice asked.

"No," the warden said. "She doesn't know anything. She has been sanctioned for stealing the cell phone, so she's been given extra work detail. She probably thinks she's to be given another job. If you need me, I'll be in my office."

August thanked the warden then watched as Bruce put some distance between him and the door and began to pace a little. Alice took a seat at the table and looked at August. "He's really wired," she mentioned, glancing over at Bruce. "Was his relationship with his mother always so strained?"

"He doesn't talk about it much," August said. "I know more about her relationship with Clay than with Bruce. I know when I suggested that she was trying to warn him about something . . . protect him, he didn't believe that."

"Must be horrible, not feeling like your mother will protect you," Al said.

August glanced over at Bruce. He was running his hand through his fair hair, staring out the window. The sound of footsteps coming down the hallway caused all three of them to look expectantly at the door.

Evelyn Monkton had aged since August last saw her, aged far beyond her forty-four years. Her hair had gone gray, and her face was carved with lines. Her mouth opened into an O when she saw her son.

Bruce came forward. He stood at August's shoulder, and Al stood up, presenting a united front.

"Hello, Mother," Bruce said.

"Mrs. Monkton," August added. "This is Alice Comeau. She works for the Manchester police, and you do remember me, don't you?"

"August," she said, entwining her hands. The guard stood behind her. August nodded at her, and she left the room. When the door closed behind the guard, Evelyn Monkton jumped. She turned and stared at the closed door.

"Mrs. Monkton . . ." August said, "Evelyn, please sit down."

Her gaze was on her son. "What are you doing here?"

"We need to talk to you," Bruce said.

"You don't care about me," she accused. "You came because of the messages."

"Yes," Bruce said, moving around the table and pulling out a chair.

August pulled out a chair for Evelyn as Al took a seat. "Please?" August said.

"I . . . I can't tell you anything," she said, taking a few steps back. "I . . . I don't know anything."

"If you'd sit down, Evelyn," August insisted.

Cautiously, she moved to the chair and sat, her gaze again returning to her son.

August took a chair. "So, how have you been?"

"You don't care." She looked at him. "You didn't come here for that."

"We do care," August said.

"It's not easy," Al spoke up, "to have a son and lose him

like that, a son who wasn't well."

Evelyn glanced at her. "Do you have children?"

"I did. I had a son who died a few months after he was born."

"I'm sorry," Evelyn said.

August looked at Al. She'd never told him that.

"You never get over losing a child," Al continued.

"Your instinct is always to protect them from harm." Evelyn nodded and looked at her hands.

August looked over at Bruce. He was worried about how he was coping. He wasn't sure what was going on inside him, but his face showed a lot of emotion.

Bruce met his gaze. August smiled at him, wishing he was close enough to hold his hand.

"You tried to protect Bruce, didn't you, Evelyn?" Alice insisted.

"Only a mother could understand that," Evelyn replied.

"What were you trying to protect him from?" August asked.

"No." She shook her head. "No, I can't." She stood up, pushing over the chair.

The guard walked in.

August shooed her away, indicating that it was alright.

"You can't what?" August asked her. "Evelyn, if you don't tell us, we can't protect Bruce."

"What does it mean, Mother?" Bruce stood and went around the table. "What does it mean? What should I be afraid of? Who will hurt me?"

Tears blurred her eyes, and she backed up again. "No, they'll kill me. They'll kill me!" she screamed.

August took hold of her shoulders. She gazed up at him with terror-filled eyes. "They? Who are they? Who are they, Mrs. Monkton?" He shook her a little.

Bruce put out his hand. "August, let her go."

August released her. She was shaking. What wouldn't she say? Who was she so afraid of?

"Tell me, Mother," Bruce said, touching her arm. "What are you trying to tell me?"

Tears ran down her face. "You think I never did right by you. You think I loved him more. I was trying to protect you. It was too late for Clay. Sometimes no one could tell you apart. I sacrificed him, Bruce," she said with a sob, "for you. But there's nowhere to hide anymore. Please, Bruce." She grabbed him by the shirt and pressed her face against his chest. "Get away from here. Get away from Blood Pond."

"Why? What are you afraid of?" August demanded.

He pulled Bruce away and took hold of her again. "No one can get to you here, Evelyn. For once in your life, do the right thing. Young men are dying. Your son might be in danger. I can't protect him if I don't know from whom."

Evelyn was crying hard now. There were no words and no confessions. Alice was there, trying to comfort her as Bruce stood by helplessly, tears in his eyes.

"Leave me alone!" she screamed. "Leave me alone!"

August called for the guard. August pointed at her as the guard took her arm. "Let it be on your conscience, Evelyn, if I find another head in Blood Pond."

August brushed past her. "Take her back to her cell," he bellowed and walked out of the room.

Alice sighed. "Coming?" she asked Bruce as his mother fell silent, her tears drying on her face.

Bruce looked at the guard then said to Alice. "Give me another minute alone with her, please? I'll be out in a minute," he told her.

Alice nodded at him and left the room.

The guard stood beside the door.

"Mother," Bruce said gently, "there's so much I don't understand. I want this to be over." The tears in his eyes spilled onto his face. "I'm so tired of living with this, fearing what I can't see, but knowing it's out there. What is it? Why can't you tell me?"

She shook her head. "I can't. Please, Bruce, I told you to get out. That's enough. Why don't you go?"

"I can't go. I can't go until it's over. Please? I have a great job now, and I have the man I love most in the world. I need to leave this behind. Will it never be over?"

She looked down again.

"Fine," he said. "Do as you always have. Leave me to fend for myself. Clay is dead, Mother, but I'm alive." He waited, misery washing over him. "Fine, goodbye, Mother."

Just as he walked past, Evelyn Monkton reached out and grabbed his arm. She drew him close and whispered in his ear. "Be careful, they're all around you."

Bruce's eyes widened. He wanted to respond, but she pushed away and quickly left the room. The guard followed.

Bruce hurried out of the room, too. He stood frozen in the hallway, her words in his head. He could see her walking away in the distance. "Who is all around me?" he yelled. "Mother. Who are they? Who in the hell are they?"

The electronic partition opened and closed, and Evelyn Monkton was lost from his view.

CHAPTER THIRTEEN

August had spoken to the warden before he left, asking her if Evelyn Monkton had received any visitors, had she been withdrawn, behaving in some way which seemed unusual?

The warden looked him in the eye. "I'm not supposed to disclose personal information," she said, "but I will tell you, Detective Greystone, I have the impression that she is gradually losing her mind. She is paranoid, often fearful, has bad dreams."

"Does she get visitors?"

"Not a one and she never uses the pay phone."

"Mail?"

"Funny you should ask. She never did before, but just recently, she received one letter, a rather strange one."

"How recently?" August asked.

"About a week ago."

"Do you know from where?"

"No return address." The warden reached in her drawer and drew out an envelope, "But it was postmarked Whitefield. I took it out and put it aside when I knew you were coming. I almost forgot about it to tell you the truth." She handed it to him.

August turned the envelope over in his hand.

"The letter doesn't make much sense, although it seems harmless enough. I was about to give it back to her when I heard about that boy turning up in Blood Pond."

"So, Evelyn has seen this letter?" August withdrew it

from the envelope.

"Yes."

"How did she react?"

"Frightened. When she was asked about it, she just withdrew."

"Can I take it with me?" She nodded.

August read the words carefully. There was a poem by Robert Burns called 'I Murder Hate' then a series of quotations, most of them misogynists' quips about women.

"What do you make of it?" the warden asked.

August put the letter back into the envelope. "Obviously someone is sending her a message, someone who doesn't like her, or women, very much. Thank you, warden," he said, shaking her hand, "you've been most helpful. I'll get my people on this letter and get it back to you when we're finished."

Everybody was quiet on the way home. August wasn't sure what was going on with Bruce. He hadn't said a word since they'd left the prison. Alice was writing notes on her laptop, observations about Evelyn Monkton. August could have summed that up with one word: terrified . . . but terrified of what . . . of whom?

"Each woman is Eve throughout the ages," August mused as he drove back to Whitefield.

"What did you say?" Alice asked, closing her notebook.

"Oh," August said, "did I just say something aloud?"

"You did, and something quite horrible about women."

"Oh, sorry, it's a quote by Meredith, one of the quotes in the letter Evelyn Monkton received."

"Can I see that?" Alice asked.

"Yeah," August replied, reaching down beside his seat and handing her the envelope. "I was going to show you back at the hotel."

"This is probably the first real lead we've had," she said,

taking it out and opening the page.

"That's what I'm thinking, too," August said, glancing back at Bruce in the mirror. "Are you hungry, Bruce?"

No answer. He'd gone off into his own little world again.

Alice glanced at August. August shrugged. "We're almost home," he said to Alice. "We'll stop at the diner." He glanced back at Bruce, who was staring straight ahead. Damn. Maybe it had been a mistake taking him to the prison.

Alice read the letter silently as August drove. He looked over at her a few times, anxious to see what she thought.

When she finally looked up from the letter, her expression was dark. "In wars at home, I'll spend my blood? What the fuck?" she mouthed.

"My sentiments exactly."

"That line was underlined. How about this one, a quote from Richardson, from Clarissa Harlowe. 'Cunning women and witches we read of without number, but wisdom never entered into the character of a woman. It is not a requisite of her sex.' Now why in the hell would someone send something like that to Evelyn Monkton? Obviously, a message but . . ." She shook her head.

"Did you read the quote from Thomas Robson?"

"Oh, yeah," Al muttered, glancing at the page again. "The one that goes, 'Even when our Mother Eve was given the best man ever made, she chose a devil for a confidant and treated the salvation of her race as a matter for a bargain counter . . .'"

"That's the one."

"The entire thing basically screams I hate women and I hate you."

August looked at Alice for a moment then turned his attention back to the road. The sign for Whitefield flashed before them.

"August, why don't you go back to the hotel with Bruce?" Alice suggested. "Drop me off at the diner. I'll bring you guys back some food, or you can meet me there later."

"Good idea," he said. "Maybe we'll join you there later." He said it, but he didn't believe it, not in the state Bruce was in.

Twenty minutes later, he dropped Al off at the diner then continued to the hotel. When he'd parked the vehicle, he got out and crawled into the back beside Bruce. "Are you going to talk to me, or just tune me out?"

"You could have gone with Alice. I'm okay," Bruce said, but he didn't look at him.

"You don't seem okay," August replied, relieved that he was finally speaking.

Bruce looked at him now. "My mother said something to me before I left that room."

"What did she say?"

"They were all around me."

"They? Bruce, I think your mother may be . . ."

Bruce shook his head. "That's just it, August, I've been remembering things, pieces of things, voices, laughter. Clay was there; *he* was there. Clay was afraid. I know that now. The fear I felt was his, too. And that someone chasing me through the woods wanted to find me, has been looking for me all this time. He knows I'm here, and that's why he's here."

"Who?"

Bruce stroked August's cheek. "We have to leave here, or something terrible is going to happen. They have us, like rats in a trap."

"They? Bruce, Clay is dead."

"Not Clay, *him, him*, August, and he's not alone." Bruce opened the door. "Listen, I don't want talk anymore. You don't believe me anyway."

"Believe what exactly?"

"Never mind. Why don't you go eat with your friend? I just want to be alone."

August watched him get out and walk to the hotel entrance. He sat back against the seat, his eyes closed.

A firm rapping on the glass caused his eyelids to fly open a few minutes later. Desmond peered in on him. "What are you doing sitting alone in the back seat?"

August reached for the door handle and got out. He could see the back of Desmond's cruiser around the side of the hotel. "I needed a minute."

"Where's Bruce?" He glanced around.

"Inside. Don't worry. He didn't run off."

"So, what happened at the prison? Did she say anything we can use?"

"Not much. We'll have a meeting tomorrow."

"She give you any names, any idea of what could be happening, why she sent those messages to your boy there?"

"No." August stretched and yawned.

"You look tired. Want to get a beer?"

He was tempted to say yes because he just didn't want to walk into that hotel room and talk in riddles with Bruce anymore. He shrugged. "Why not? I haven't eaten yet either. They still make those good burgers at the bar?"

"Sure do," Desmond said. "Come on, buddy, we'll take the cruiser."

Bruce watched August walk across the parking lot with Desmond Johnson. He clutched the material of the curtain in his hand, only realizing how tight his grip was when a part of the curtain ripped off in his hand. *He will leave you soon. Who will you have? You will be alone. Desmond is so much better for him than you. They have more in common, more to talk about, and he doesn't walk around filled with fear and anxiety all the time. You're a loser, a basketcase who hears voices, imagines shadows coming to take you away. They should lock you up again.* "August," he gasped, "don't. Don't go."

"Darcy French stood out," Desmond replied when August inquired about how the interviews were going.

"How so?"

Desmond chomped down on his burger. He wiped his mouth with the napkin as the waitress brought them a pitcher of beer. "Thanks, hot stuff," he said.

August sat back in his chair, waiting for an answer.

"He's thirty-nine, still lives with his mother, never had a girlfriend. You know the kind."

August nodded. "That doesn't make him a killer," August said, "although he fits the profile of someone in the closet, maybe even someone who likes young boys." He picked up his burger and took a bite.

"He was nervous when we interviewed him, a little evasive. Asked him why he volunteers at the high school so much, and he said he likes sports."

"What does he do for a living?"

"He works at the arena in the winter, takes care of the ice. In the summer, he does odd jobs. Don't think he's that bright."

"Is he developmentally delayed?"

"He attended special class as a kid. Wouldn't call him retarded though, maybe borderline. We can get a specialist to look at him if you like."

"Anything concrete? Evidence that puts him at the scene or . . ." August took another bite of his burger as he looked at Desmond.

"Not yet." He grinned. "Give me time."

"That's the problem, Des," August replied, sipping his beer. "We don't have a lot of that. Affleck is breathing down my neck. He sent me three emails today. He wants another report."

Desmond finished off his burger. He poured them both another glass of beer and stayed quiet as August finished the rest of his meal. "Coleslaw is good," August commented.

"Yeah," Desmond agreed, "they make it fresh. This is nice, just like old times."

Like old times, August thought. Did he and Des have any 'old times'?

"Remember when we were at the academy?" August nodded.

"Remember when I invited you to spend the weekend with me, and you went off with that new training officer, what was his name . . . Paul—"

"Doesn't matter, Des," August said, cutting him off. "That was long time ago."

"I still remember it." Desmond's voice grew angrier as he went on. "I really thought we had something, thought that you were going to spend that weekend with me, and instead you spent it fucking that cocky, hotshot from . . . Where in hell was he from? New York?"

"Desmond, what is this all about? Did you bring me here for this?"

"While you were fucking him, your brother was getting his head cut off." He laughed and met August's horrified gaze. "I hope to hell that bastard was good."

August sat back in his seat as if someone had stuck a machete in him. He melted against the seat, his throat working.

"Don't look so shocked." Desmond shrugged his broad shoulders. "Someone needed to say it, didn't they? And instead of learning your lesson, you're doing the same thing again. You let Tommy down, August. You came close to finding a killer the last time, and you got distracted by a sweet little blond angel with a firm ass, an angel with a black heart."

"You fucking son of a bitch," August said under his
breath. He wasn't sure if he was saying it about himself or
about Desmond. He looked up, met Desmond's self-assured
gaze, and swallowed the pain those words caused him deep
inside. "I almost forgave you for the last time, the last stu-
pidity that came out of your mouth. We were getting along
fine again and you . . . Why? I don't understand what's happened to you, Desmond."

"What's happened to me? What's happened to you, August? I admitted my mistakes. I missed my opportunity with
you. I was a coward who hid in the closet when I should
have just taken hold of you and made you mine when I had
the chance. Now I've admitted that. You admit your mistakes. You betrayed me, led me on, made me think there was
something . . . fucked me so . . ." He stopped. "Then you
went off with him, and you were punished for that."

"Punished? Desmond, there was nothing between us except a few nights of rough sex, that's it. I made no promises
to you."

"But I've changed."

August leaned across the table. "I love Bruce."

"You're a fool. He's no good for you."

"So be it." August sat back in the chair.

"At least you admit he wasn't your best decision, August,
that you can never really be sure about him. Don't tell me
you've never had doubts deep in your gut."

August sighed. He looked around the bar. It was almost
empty. "Doesn't everyone have doubts about everything?"

"Even if Bruce didn't wield the weapon that cut off that
boy's head, he's involved. That boy was killed because Bruce
came back to town. Look at me and deny it. Come on, August, lie to yourself again. It's easy when you're lying next to
him, isn't it?"

Yes, it's easy, damn easy.

"You can blame me all you want, my friend, but someone has got to make you see the truth," Desmond said. "Come on, let's order another pitcher and forget this shit for a while." He reached across and briefly touched his hand then called for the waitress to bring another pitcher.

There had been a car sitting in the parking lot outside the hotel for the last hour. Every once in a while, the high beams came on, then cut out. There was someone sitting in the driver's seat, but it was too dark for Bruce to make out who it was. No one had gotten in or out of the vehicle.

Bruce went back to the window every ten minutes to look. It was still there. He picked up the hotel phone, dialed an outside line, and punched in August's phone number. He put the receiver down on the first ring. August would think he was being paranoid again, not to mention that he was probably pissed at him for his behavior earlier. Where in the hell was he anyway? He'd gone off with Desmond two hours ago.

When he went to the window and saw the car again, he left his room and went next door to see Al. He knocked three times, but there was no answer. She hadn't come back yet either. Maybe she was with August and Desmond. Bruce returned to his room and sat down on the edge of the bed, vowing not to go back to the window. Whoever was in that car, it probably had nothing to do with him. He'd be patient and wait. He was sure August would be back soon. He began to relax, telling himself everything was alright. There was nothing out there in the night waiting to get him.

Then the phone rang.

"I have to take a piss," August muttered, pushing up from

the table. He'd already drunk way too much. It was time to go back to the hotel.

Desmond was chuckling. "Can I hold it?"

August pushed Desmond's hand away as he stumbled past the table. "Get out of here."

"Playing hard to get, eh? I got to go, too."

August stood in front of the urinal, Desmond beside him. His head was spinning. The beer combined with the exhaustion was taking its toll. His did up his pants, aware that Desmond's gaze had been centered on his dick, and patted his pockets.

Desmond did up his pants, too. He crowded August against the wall. "What are you looking for, baby?"

August gave him a little push. "I'm not your baby, and where in hell did I put my phone?"

"You probably left it back in your car."

"Damn it," August said. "Lend me yours." He held out his hand. "I should call Bruce."

"Sure," he said with a laugh, "anything for you." Desmond placed both palms on August's chest. "Kiss me."

"No, Des." August shook his head. "Stop. We're both drunk. Cut it out."

"Just one kiss," he pleaded, his mouth seeking August's.

August gave him one good shove. "I said no."

Desmond stood some distance away, his expression hardening. "Fine," he replied. "Come on, let's get you back to your precious little fuckhole."

"I can get to the hotel by myself," August told him. "I'll walk."

"It's dark, and at least ten minutes by foot. I'll take you," Desmond insisted, following August outside.

August turned and looked at him. "You're lucky I'm drunk, Des. If I wasn't, I would have kicked your ass in there. Don't you ever do that again."

"You're overreacting. August," he called out as August began to walk.

"Where in fuck is my phone," he muttered as he trudged back toward the hotel. He wouldn't have left the hotel without it.

The walk turned out to be a good thing though. He'd pretty well sobered up by the time he arrived back at the hotel.

He searched his car in the parking lot but didn't find his phone. "Damn! Fuck!" He couldn't lose his phone. He was in a bad mood when he walked into the hotel room. When he saw Bruce's face, he tried to hide his frustration. "Hey, are you alright?"

Bruce shook his head. "August, there was someone in a car watching the hotel, and then I got these calls, and there was no one on the other end, and I tried to call you after that, but I just got your voice mail—"

"Hold on, slow down," August said, his head pounding. "Who was watching the hotel?"

"I don't know. Someone in a car."

"Someone in a car, in the parking lot?" He sighed. "Bruce, it could have been anyone in that car. Why do you think they were watching you?"

"I just know they were watching me. Then I got these calls, just breathing. August, we got to leave here. I'm so scared."

August pulled him into his arms. *He's sick, August. Bruce is sick.*

"You've been drinking," Bruce said, pulling away.

"A little bit."

"With Desmond Johnson."

"Yes."

"Al wasn't with you?"

"No. She went to eat."

"She's not in her room."

89

August narrowed his eyes. "She should be back. What's her cell phone number? Fuck."

"It's in your phone," Bruce said.

"I've lost my phone."

"Lost your phone?"

"You heard me, Bruce," he snapped. "I lost my phone." August tore out of the room and banged on the room next door. "Al? Al, you in there?"

No answer.

"I'm going to ask them to ring her room at the front desk," he said to Bruce who'd followed him into the hallway.

"I'll come with you," Bruce offered.

The guy at the front desk rang Alice's room and handed August the phone. Ten times it rang. August handed the phone back to the desk clerk. "Did you see Alice Comeau tonight?" he asked him.

"No, sir," he said.

"Anyone else come into the hotel, any strangers?"

"Didn't see anyone," he replied. "Sorry."

"Also, I lost my cell phone. If you find one, it's probably mine, Blackberry Bold, registered to the police department."

"I'll write that down."

August went to the front door of the lobby and stepped outside. Bruce stood beside him. The parking lot was empty except for August's car, Bruce's car, and three other cars that August would verify with the desk clerk but was sure belonged to hotel guests. "The car you saw, Bruce, is it still here?"

Bruce studied the vehicles. "No."

"Tell me about the calls." He looked at him.

"I got three, none of them lasting more than a minute. Then I looked outside after the last one, and the car was gone."

"I need to look for Al."

"I'm coming," Bruce told him. "Want to split up?" he asked as they walked to the car.

August threw him the keys. "No. You stay with me, and you drive."

"Good idea," Bruce grumbled, "given the state you're in."

The main street was deserted. They stopped the vehicle at one point and walked into the diner, then toured the bar. The owner of the diner told him that Alice had been in earlier, eaten and left. "She said she was beat and was going back to the hotel to sleep," the man said.

"Thanks." August frowned. "Can I use your phone?"

"Sure."

August called police dispatch and asked to be connected to his department. Affleck wasn't there, thank God. Doug Anderson was the officer on duty and was reputed to be far more understanding.

"We'll send a phone down to you pronto, August. And are you sure Al has gone missing?"

"I'm worried. Can you give me her cell phone number?"

"Sure," he said, "hold on."

August wrote it on a napkin when Anderson rattled it off a few minutes later. "This is not like her. This is a hard town to hide in, and she's like nowhere."

"We'll send a courier to the hotel. You should have your phone in three hours or so. Is there anything you want me to tell the captain?"

"Not yet. I'll call him tomorrow."

"Keep us posted, August."

"Sure." He hung up then called Alice's cell phone number. The phone rang four times then the answering machine kicked in. August hung up.

"She's not answering her cell," August announced as the two men stood on the deserted main street, looking up and down for any sign of movement. The town was dead, and the warm air was almost stifling. Only the sign from the bar flashed hopelessly on and off.

Bruce touched his arm. "We'll find her, August."

"I hope so."

They walked back to the car, and sat there in the front seat, not talking for a while. Bruce knew that August was deep in thought. "What are you thinking?" he asked finally.

August sighed. "I'm thinking that you were at the hotel and maybe you saw her."

Bruce paled. "What? You think I did something to Alice?"

August put his face in his hands. "I don't know anything anymore. I want off this fucking case. I should have never taken it on. I'm in over my head, and maybe Desmond is right." He looked at Bruce. "I don't really know you at all."

Bruce's mouth dropped. "August," he whispered, swallowing hard.

"I have no perspective," August shook his head. "Because I'm fucking the only real suspect we have in this case, and I feel surrounded by . . . It feels like everyone in this God-damned town is involved in this shit."

Bruce nodded without saying anything. What could he say? He couldn't blame him. "I've been waiting for that."

"Bruce, I . . ." August reached out for him.

"No, it's alright." Bruce shook his head. He opened the car door and looked back at him. "This was too good to be true, you and me. I knew eventually it would come to an end. You don't trust me and yet you trust Desmond." He got out, shut the car door and started walking up the street.

August sat back for a moment, closing his eyes. "Damn,

what did I say?" He turned in his seat. Bruce had disappeared. He scrambled out of the car and frantically scanned the area. "Bruce," he called out. "I didn't mean it. Bruce!" He ran around to the driver's side and slid into the seat. He reached for the keys. Nothing.

"Damn." Bruce had taken the keys with him.

Bruce walked at a fast pace up the road, his eyes blurred with tears. He wanted to get to the hotel, pack his bags, and do what he had originally done when all this began—get away, run, and never stop. If it hadn't been for August seeking him out, he would have never come back to this place. Now he was thinking that he'd fallen for August the first time he'd laid eyes on that picture Tommy had shown him.

When he heard the car in the distance, he turned around. His heart lifted, thinking August had come after him. He'd make everything better. Maybe they'd just leave here together, never come back. *I love you, August.* But then he felt the car keys in his pocket.

He turned, prepared to head back and give August a lift to the hotel when the car approached, the headlights practically blinding him. For a moment, he panicked then he relaxed some when he saw the police cruiser. Desmond drove up beside him. "Where you going, Bruce? Running again?"

Bruce regarded Desmond from a distance. The panic in his gut rose again. He didn't approach the vehicle, and suddenly, he wanted to run. "I'm . . . ah . . . August is close by. He'll be along any minute. I . . . ."

"Did you have a lover's squabble?" He grinned at him.

"No. I . . . I've got to get to him. He doesn't have the keys, and he's waiting so . . ." Bruce turned around in the other direction.

The car door opened and Desmond got out. Bruce took a

step backward, almost falling. He recovered his footing just in time for Desmond to grab him by the arm and pull him up to his chest. "He's here, and he's been waiting a long time for you, Bruce."

Bruce struggled, but Desmond held him fast.

He began to drag him toward the cruiser as Bruce struggled to get free. "Honey boy, I'm not going to hurt you, but I'm afraid that poor August is just going to have to find his own way home tonight."

CHAPTER FOURTEEN

"Don't know where he is right now," Joe said. "He'll probably be around soon. Good thing you stopped by. I tried to call you tonight."

August barely heard the officer's words. He felt as if he was in the Twilight Zone. When he'd gotten back to the hotel, Alice still wasn't there, and now, neither was Bruce. When he walked into the hotel room, and Bruce's clothes were still in the closet, his stomach tightened. He demanded that the clerk open Al's room. All her stuff was there, too, but there was no sign of a struggle. She'd even taken the time to lock her door.

August told the desk clerk that he was expecting a parcel and to leave it at the desk, then he'd headed to the police station. Now this cop was telling him something that he couldn't quite wrap his head around. "What did you say?"

"We got a report on another missing boy, Peter Ludlow. His parents are in the interrogation room now."

"Peter Ludlow? Dennis Jameson's best friend?"

"That's the one."

"How long has he been missing?" Nothing felt real. All this stuff floating around in his head, and he was desperately trying to make some sense out of it. Now, three people were missing.

"Never came back from school today," Joe said.

"Shit," August muttered as he walked into the conference room.

The Ludlows had both been crying, and their daughter sat

in the corner with her head down. She'd already experienced enough trauma. Now her brother was gone.

"Detective." Mr. Ludlow jumped from his seat. "Did you find our boy?"

"No, I've only just found out he was missing. You need to tell me everything," he said, propelling the man back into his seat. "Has your son ever done anything like this before, taken off and not told you where he'd gone?" Both the Ludlows shook their heads.

Peter's sister looked up and said, "Peter is a bit of a square. He'd never go off like that without telling someone."

Suddenly, Desmond walked in. He reached out right away to the Ludlows, took their hands and held them a good long while. "Try not to worry. I'm sure he's just messing around somewhere."

The Ludlows had no useful information to impart besides the fact that Peter left school at the same time he usually did and then never showed up at home. His sister had seen him once during the day but had to stay after school, so she had no idea when he'd left. They'd called some of his friends, and none of them had seen him after the school bell.

"Desmond, can I talk to you?" August took his elbow and steered him out the door and into the hallway. "Alice Comeau is gone and so is Bruce. I'm really worried. Bruce said someone had been watching the hotel and that he'd received strange phone calls. Al never came back after eating at the diner."

"Bruce took off? That little . . . Well, I expected he'd run the first chance he got."

"No, he's missing. If he'd tried to run, his clothes would be gone from the room and so would his car. Everything is still there."

"He wouldn't have had time to pack, not if he was in a hurry and he knew you could arrive at any moment. Now we have another missing boy on our hands. Think about it, August. Bruce could have killed Al. Maybe she was onto him. She told me she never trusted him. She told me she thought Bruce was involved. Now, will you please accept that your judgment has been clouded?" He put a hand on August's shoulder. "It happens to the best of us, my friend."

August shook his head.

"There's no other explanation. Come on, we need to look for Peter Ludlow. Maybe he's just run off with some cute little chick, and he's banging her up at Blood Pond.

Joe," Desmond called out, "stay with the Ludlows."

August went outside and over to Desmond's cruiser. *Bruce a murderer? No. I'll never believe that. I'll never believe that Bruce, my Bruce, could hurt anyone, and yet, in a moment of frustration, I basically told Bruce I didn't trust him anymore.*

"Oh," Desmond said as August climbed in the squad car beside him, "by the way, I found your cell phone." He reached beside him and handed it to him."

"Where'd you find it?"

"You dropped it in the bar. Barmaid called me. She's hot for me, you know."

August hardly heard him, his thoughts were on Al and Bruce and Peter Ludlow. He wasn't optimistic where this kid was concerned. *Please let me save just one of them. Bruce . . . Bruce, where in the hell are you?*

Desmond raised a hand as August thanked him then they careened out of town, taking the road that led to Blood Pond.

The house wasn't that far from August's old house, although it sat back from the water some. Surrounded by trees, it was isolated and practically soundproof. *So, no one can hear you scream.*

A young boy of around fifteen or so lay on a faded carpet

in the middle of the living room floor. He'd been tied, hands to ankles, his mouth covered with the same tape plastered over Bruce's mouth. The boy struggled and looked at Bruce with pleading eyes.

Bruce wanted to comfort him, but how? It was all he could do not to lose it himself, tied to a chair, listening for every sound.

He couldn't believe what had just happened. Desmond had slapped handcuffs on him and thrown him into the back seat. Bruce had thought he was taking him to jail and now here he was, a prisoner. "You have nothing on me," Bruce had hollered angrily at him from the back seat. "August will kick your ass."

He laughed. "I don't think we'll have to worry about August, at least you won't." Desmond did a U-turn in the middle of the road.

Bruce narrowed his eyes. "Hey, this isn't the way to town."

"No," he said, "it isn't."

"Where are you . . . take-taking me?"

"To visit the queen." He laughed.

"Desmond, fuck. Where are you taking me?"

Desmond glared at him through his mirror. "Where you won't be a nuisance, where you'll do what you were supposed to fucking do . . . away from August." He smiled. "August is mine now."

"Fuck you!"

"We'll see," he said.

When they rounded the lake and drove down the dirt road to the house in the wooded area, Bruce was confused. "What is this place?"

Desmond came around and dragged Bruce out of the back seat. "Your time for asking questions is over." Desmond pushed him hard against the squad car, stuck his gun under his chin then plastered the heavy tape over his mouth. "There, that's better."

When Desmond shoved Bruce inside the front door of the house, and he saw that boy, he was stunned. The boy cried out under the tape. It sounded as if someone was strangling him. *Oh no, God, not another one. Was Desmond the murderer? Couldn't have been him who killed Tommy. He was away at the police academy with August when Tommy died.*

Desmond didn't say anything as he roughly bound Bruce to the chair and left him alone in that room with the boy on the carpet.

He sat there for what seemed like forever, a clock on the mantel ticking away the minutes. Then the door to the other room opened, and a man stood there. He was in his thirties maybe, balding, wearing horn-rimmed glasses.

"Hello, Bruce," he said. "Sorry we had to do this. You'll be loose soon enough. My name is Darcy. I'm pleased to finally meet you, Bruce." He walked over and ran a hand over Bruce's hair. "You are beautiful." Bruce tried to shake off his hand.

The man called Darcy walked over to where the boy lay. "I hate to see them like that. Don't worry," he said, leaning down to pat the boy on the shoulder, "we'll take care of you." Darcy looked at Bruce. "He's cuter than the last one."

Bruce swallowed, sweat running down his temples. *Please, God. August.* He closed his eyes. *Will I ever see you again?*

When Bruce heard footsteps approach, Darcy quickly moved from the boy on the floor. He stood against the wall, looking a little stressed, his hands clutching on to one another. The footsteps grew closer.

Bruce looked up to see a man standing in the doorway. He was blond and movie-star handsome. A huge smile spread across his face.

"Bruce," he exclaimed, stepping over the struggling figure on the floor.

Bruce's stomach began to heave, the fear so intense he thought he was going to pass out. Flashes of Clay and him as boys playing in the bedroom . . . heavy footsteps approaching . . . frozen in fear.

Bruce, hide, hide, he's coming. Help us, Mommy! The door burst open, and a tall man stood there with a strap in hand, a smile on his face. Get those pants down, boys. You've been bad, really bad.

The man in front of him smiled and reached down now, caressing his cheek. He glanced at Darcy. "Isn't he pretty, Darcy?"

"Beautiful, Bruce, he's just beautiful, a chip off the old block he is."

The man's blue eyes gazed into Bruce's. "You don't know how happy I am to see you again, son."

"What in hell are we doing out here?" August demanded as he stood out in the middle of the road near Blood Pond. "We should organize a search party."

"But I know all the make-out spots. You remember being that age, don't you, August, with hormones raging?" Desmond came closer, lowered his voice seductively. "Do the hormones still rage, baby?"

August narrowed his eyes. He gave him a shove. "Desmond, why didn't you call out a search party?"

"I told you. Chances are the kid is up here getting his rocks off with some blonde chick . . . or blond stud?" He winked, reaching for him again.

He shoved Desmond's hand away as the other man tried to touch his face. "Come on, Des, no time for that now. We need to find Peter. Give me your phone. I'll call headquarters, and we'll get a search party up here. We can't comb these woods alone."

"We don't need one," Desmond said, looking at him.

"Is that so?" August demanded, and instinctively put his hand on his gun.

Bruce's mind suddenly began to clear. He hadn't realized that he'd lost consciousness. When he raised his head, he was still tied to the chair, but the tape was gone. The boy who'd been on the floor was missing, and so was the weird-looking guy with the geeky glasses.

The tall, blond man was still there though. He stood at the mantel, staring into what was now a small fire.

"Where is he?" Bruce demanded. He barely dared breathe. "Where is that boy?"

The man turned and smiled at him. "Ah, you've come back to me."

Bruce told himself to be strong. He raised his chin and met his gaze. "You can't hurt me anymore."

"Can't I?"

Those two words went right through him.

"Bruce," he said softly, "I don't want to hurt you. I want you with me. That she-bitch mother of yours deprived me all those years of my boys, my children." His voice sounded plaintive. "The fruit of my loins. She's lucky I didn't kill her for that."

Tears filled Bruce's eyes. He blinked them away. "What do you want with me?"

"I want us to ride the waves of glory together, son. I want to teach you the power, show you the supreme pleasure, give you the benefits of my wisdom."

"I . . . I don't want anything from you. You killed Tommy. You murdered others, and you forced Clay to help you do it." Bruce shook his head. Bitterly, he said, "You even have a fucking fan club, don't you? Desmond, that cop that brought me here, and that spaz that was in here before, and God knows who else. Pedophiles, all of them, worshipping at the great master's feet."

He smiled. "Bruce, you're so smart. You were always smarter than Clay. That's why he loved you so."

The tears spilled down Bruce's cheeks now. Clay had protected him when they were children, shielded him from some of the abuse, the sexual torture. He could still hear him screaming if he closed his eyes. He'd pushed that so far down inside of him. He had blocked it out totally, but now . . . the monster was here, right in front of him.

"You destroyed him," Bruce whispered. "You abused him so much that Mother had to lock him away."

"She kept him from me!" he bellowed, advancing on the chair. "She had no right!"

Bruce squeezed his eyes shut. He couldn't look at that face, all animated with fury. That's why they'd moved around so much, that's why she was always so afraid, why she couldn't put Clay away for good. It would mean they'd have to stay in one place, and she couldn't risk that.

"Bruce Monkton." Bruce opened his eyes.

The man had returned to the fireplace, seemingly mesmerized by the fire dancing there. He glanced at him.

"You signed your own name when you camped at Roger's, but it was like a joke, wasn't it?"

He laughed. "Yes. You'd forgotten about me. How could you forget your own father?"

"And Tommy . . ." He swallowed. "Why Tommy?"

"Because you cared more for him than for your own blood. Clay felt it too. You abandoned him."

"No," Bruce cried out. "I wanted a life. You had no right to take his life. He did nothing to you. And all those others . . . Why?"

"Because I can." He shrugged. "And so, can you. You will

102

be everything Clay never could be, Bruce." He marched over to the chair and began to untie him. "I'm going to show you everything."

Bruce struggled as the man pulled him to his feet. The door opened, and another man stood there, older, portly.

"Hello, coach," Bruce Monkton said. "Meet my son, my clone, Bruce Monkton."

The portly man smiled as he approached. "Fine looking young man," he said, "a little too old for me though."

"He's not fodder," Monkton said then looked at his son. "He's my apprentice."

The woman pulled her housecoat around her and backed up when August barreled through the doorway. "Where's your son?"

"I . . . I don't know." She shook her head. "In bed, I think. I . . . I . . . don't—"

August didn't give her time to respond. He withdrew his gun. "Darcy, Darcy French, police." He searched every room and then found the basement door. He hurried down the steps. There was a small office, a desk, a laptop. He picked up the laptop and ran back upstairs. "If he comes back," August said, "you call this number."

"What's he done?" she cried. "What do you want with my little boy?"

August threw the laptop into the back seat of Desmond's cruiser and screeched back out onto the road. He was following his gut instead of his head, and if he was wrong, he'd probably lose his job for abandoning the Whitefield chief of police out at Blood Pond.

On the way to Coach Richardson's house, he called the police station. Joe answered. "Detective. I did what you told me," he said. "I got a bunch of people together for the search party. Desmond called. He's hopping mad of course. I told him that someone would give him a lift back. Didn't say I saw you."

"Good. You didn't call French or Richardson for the search, right?"

"Nope."

"Okay, sit tight, and thanks." He hung up and concentrated on the road.

He felt as if he'd gone a little crazy, and he'd reacted without taking a long time to think about it. There was something odd about Desmond's behavior out at Blood Pond. In fact, he'd been acting a little weird for some time but dragging him out there alone to look for a missing boy, given the history of Blood Pond, was not even coming close to following police procedures. August got the impression that Desmond was trying to distract him, waste his time.

Peter Ludlow had not taken anyone out to Blood Pond to neck in the woods. The kid would have had to be nuts given that his friend had just been murdered out there, and this kind of behavior, according to his parents, was not in his nature.

Desmond knew that, yet he insisted that the Ludlow kid had gone out there on some romantic adventure.

August had played along, suggesting they split up to search. The moment Desmond was far enough away, August made a dash for the police car and jumped behind the wheel. He knew Desmond had left the keys in the car.

As August drove off down the road, he could hear Desmond yelling, but he couldn't see him for his dust.

Coach Richardson's house was dark. He'd always been a bachelor and lived alone. August took French's laptop out of the back seat and walked up to the front door of Richardson's small bungalow. He knocked. No answer. He tried the door then took off his jacket, covered his arm and smashed the glass.

If what he suspected was true, he'd have Whitefield crawling with police from Manchester by tomorrow morning.

The coach's house was dark. He switched on a lamp and glanced around the living room, which was furnished with an old, threadbare sofa and a well-used La-Z-Boy. There was a small television in the corner. As August walked into the dining room and explored the kitchen, he couldn't help thinking that, for a single man with no kids, you'd think on his salary his house would be a little bit more upscale.

There was one bedroom in the back, and the bed was unmade. On the nightstand were a few sports magazines and an old family Bible. Nothing special in the drawers. Nothing special in the bathroom.

August laid French's laptop down on the sideboard and pulled on a door he assumed was a closet. It was locked. He tried the one next to it. It opened. That was the closet. The other door had to lead to the basement.

He fiddled with the handle then stood back, took out his gun and shot a hole in the door beside the handle. He descended into the basement and turned on the light. His mouth agape, he surveyed the basement contents, and he understood why the coach had shitty furniture. All his money was spent on high-tech movie equipment and computers.

August pulled out his phone and began to dial Joe, then realized he couldn't get a signal down here. He froze when he heard the sound of footsteps right above his head. August tightened the hold on his gun when he heard the door to the basement slam shut.

He raced up the stairs and pushed on the door but realized that something had been wedged against it so it wouldn't open. As he pushed on the door, his nostrils were filled with the smell of something burning. He looked down, and smoke was wafting under the door.

When the coach's cell phone played 'Take Me Out to the Ball Game,' Bruce Monkton looked over at him and demanded, "Who is it?"

The coach was still holding onto Bruce with one hand. "Desmond."

"You better take it," Monkton said. "It's okay, leave us. My son and I will be just fine."

"I'm not your son," Bruce protested as the other man pushed him forward down the hallway. He wanted to hear what Desmond was telling the coach. Was it about August? Was August okay? Did he know where he was?

Another door opened, and the older man pushed him inside. That boy lay on the bed. He'd been stripped, spread-eagled, and tied. He wasn't moving.

Bruce ran over to him. "No, no."

A hand reached out, turned him around and slapped his face hard. "Don't be such a Goddamned pussy, Bruce."

Bruce raised his hand to his face. "Don't kill him."

"I'm not going to kill him," he said. "You are."

Bruce's eyes widened, and he shook his head. "No."

"First, my friends will play a little, then when we're tired, we'll—"

"Bruce." The coach walked into the room. "Can I talk to you?"

Monkton looked angry. "Can't you see I'm having a fa-ther-son moment here? What in fuck do you want?"

"Desmond says we have trouble."

"Then tell Desmond to take care of it," Bruce Monkton said between clenched teeth. "He's a fucking policeman, isn't he?"

"I really think we . . . ." The coach looked at him.

"Anything you need to say to me, you can say in front of my beloved son. Go ahead."

Bruce bit his lip as the coach said, "Greystone went to French's house. He's also found my stuff in the basement. He knows."

"He knows about you, not about me. What's being done?"

"Desmond had someone set a fire. I'm going to lose everything, Goddamn it," the coach swore. "Do you know how much that stuff is worth? Not to mention my house?"

"Do you know what you could lose if they trace that stuff to you?" Monkton sneered. "Moron. Where in fuck is that Goddamned Manchester cop now?"

The coach smiled. "In the basement."

August raced down the stairs and hunted for any towels or blankets. He found sleazy underwear and beach towels. He pushed the stuff against the door, tucking it under the best he could.

There were two windows, narrow ones that swung out. A series of three metal bars covered each of them. "Fuck me!" he yelled. August crawled up on top of some crates to reach the window. He knew he didn't have long.

I'm sorry Bruce. If I don't get out of this alive, I hope somehow you know that.

August studied the window frames. He told himself not to panic. The windows were old and made of wood. He didn't have a hack saw to cut through the iron bars. He'd have to take out the entire frame. A crowbar would be handy at that moment, but he didn't see anything like that around.

The smell of smoke was now stronger. Maybe someone had seen the smoke and called the fire department. He jumped off the crates and searched for something to pry off the window frame.

The material blocking the opening in the door at the top of the stairs was no longer doing the job. The basement was filled with smoke. August began to cough, searching frantically for something, anything. His only thought besides survival right now was that all this evidence was going to be destroyed, and he'd even left Darcy French's laptop upstairs.

Sex toys and pornography were everywhere but not a tool in sight. Then he spotted something over in the corner he hadn't seen before, and maybe, just maybe it would help him get out of there.

"I beg you, do what you want to me, but don't hurt August," Bruce pleaded. "We can go, you and I, out of here, Father," he said, swallowing the bile as he said it.

It didn't matter anymore. It was all over, no matter what happened. His father was a serial killer. He couldn't be with August now. If he could lead this sick fuck away from here, pretend to want to join him in his insanity, the first chance he got, he'd kill the bastard in his sleep.

"Ah, son," his father said, his hand sliding up his cheek and into his hair. "You'd do anything to save that cop, wouldn't you?"

Bruce nodded frantically, shaking with fear. "Yes."

"Even lie your ass off to me." His face twisted as he clutched some of Bruce's hair and pulled hard.

Bruce winced.

"You really want to join me then let me show you the magic. Come on." He released him.

Bruce was pushed out of the room, wandering down another narrow corridor until they came to the backdoor.

"Go on," he said, pushing the door open. "Down the stairs, over to those trees."

Bruce was shaking, but he tried to keep it hidden. Only the moonlight illuminated their path and the feeling that he would die here washed over him.

"Through the trees," his father insisted.

Bruce pushed past the brush and into the woods. He glanced behind him a few times. He had a flashback. He'd run through these trees before, someone chasing him, Tommy's brutal murder playing in his mind. Clay, or was it this monster who'd chased him?

"There," his father pointed. "That's what's left of poor Dennis. I'm afraid the animals have had a go at him. It was my intention to give this one a proper burial. He didn't scream . . . much."

Bruce's stomach heaved as he looked down as a headless corpse already in a state of decay, crawling with worms and bugs, pieces of his naked body chewed or missing.

Bruce backed away, telling himself to hold onto his stomach contents, but he vomited anyway. The smell was unbearable. *You sick bastard.*

The man was saying something to him, but Bruce was hardly registering his words. His gaze returned to what was left of Dennis Jameson. *Tommy.* Tommy was all he could think of, the way he'd died, terrified, and in pain. *Madness.* He could easily descend into madness surrounded by such unthinkable horror.

"You sent the poems to Evelyn," he said suddenly, looking at his father, wiping his mouth with his hand. He took several steps away from the corpse.

"I sent one poem," he corrected. "Just to let her know I was thinking about her. She's my wife after all."

"All those years, we never stayed in one place. She was protecting us from you."

"She had no right. You are my children." The anger in his voice amplified through the trees.

Bruce closed his eyes. "Where is August?"

"Call me Dad again, and maybe I'll tell you."

"Dad." He spit out the word. "Where in fuck is my August?"

"My August . . . rather sweet. You really do love the big brute. That's why it pains me to have to tell you this. I had no choice really. Sometimes it's a disadvantage to be smart . . . too fucking smart."

"What in fucking hell did you do to August?" Bruce demanded. "Dad?"

"We had to take care of him."

The beach umbrella had a heavy, pointed tip which would allow it to be planted in the sand on a sunny day. It was solid enough so that once August jammed it securely into the crack of the wooden window frame and lifted upwards, he was able to break the frame. He used every ounce of strength he had to push out the entire window then crawled outside. He was lying on the ground when the fire department arrived.

A medic came over to give him oxygen, and someone mentioned the hospital. August pushed the mask away and shook his head, coughing. "No. No hospital." He couldn't trust anyone, not medics, or fire officials.

He sat up, ignoring the pleas of the medics, and stumbled a few feet away from the inferno that was the coach's house. He dialed his precinct in Manchester.

When Desmond pulled up in his car, August stood back a little. He watched him as he played the role of chief, assessing the situation. August tucked his cell phone into his belt and pulled out his gun. He came walking around the house, his pistol pointed directly at Desmond's forehead. "You son of a bitch. You fucking prick."

Desmond looked around him. The people standing around were staring curiously. Joe drove up now in a patrol car and parked behind Desmond's. He got out of his car.

"August. Thank God you're alright." Desmond threw up his hands.

August came closer. The gun never wavered in his hand.

"August, what's, ah, with you? He's a little stunned from the smoke, I think. Someone . . . Joe," Desmond turned and looked behind him. "Get someone to look at August."

Joe didn't move. He just stood there, his hand near his weapon.

"Hey, what's going on here?"

August stopped a few inches away, the barrel of his gun pressed into Desmond's forehead. The people gasped.

"You're under arrest."

He laughed. "For what?"

"Conspiracy to commit murder, pedophilia, attempted murder of a police officer, obstructing justice, betraying your oath as an officer of the law . . . you want more?"

"Joe," Desmond said, his face hardening, "do something. This man has lost his mind. Arrest him."

Joe moved up a few steps. He grabbed Desmond's wrist and slapped a cuff around it.

"Don't move," August shouted out as Desmond looked as if he was going to bolt.

Joe slapped on the other cuff.

"Don't plan on getting any sleep tonight Desmond," August warned as Joe led him to the police car and put him into the back seat. August followed Joe to the car. "I'm coming along with you, just to make sure old Desmond here makes it to a cell alright."

As Joe spoke with the firefighters, August remained by the car. Desmond didn't look at him, just kept his head down. A few minutes later, Joe returned to the car. "August," Joe said, "firemen managed to pull this out of the building." He handed him French's laptop. "Cover is a little melted, but it might still be of some use."

August took it with a nod of thanks as he crawled into the passenger seat. "For a day that started out shit, this might just turn out to be my lucky day."

"You need to stop sniveling," Bruce Monkton told him as he put his feet up on the table in the dining room.

If August was dead, there was no reason for him to go on, except he had to put an end to this, an end to *him*. He wished he could just shut off the flow of tears, but he couldn't. He felt the loss of August like something inside him had died. Without him, his life didn't have much meaning.

"You wouldn't understand the meaning of love, would you?" Bruce said to his father. "You only understand pain."

"Pain is pleasure, my son," he whispered. "I'm sure sex with August could sometimes get a little rough, and it hurt, but oh . . . it hurt so good." Monkton got up and began dancing around, singing 'Hurts So Good' by John Cougar. He laughed. "You're too young to remember that song. John Cougar. Wow." He sighed. "Youth."

"Why do you do it? I mean, I don't understand."

"I told you because I can. Why waste time negotiating what you want? Take it. It's a disposable world. I've been up and down this state taking what I want when I want it. And when I die, I'll go down in history. You live well and die well. Who would want anything else?"

Suddenly that little weird guy came in. He looked upset. "Bruce. My mother called me, crying. The police were there looking for me. That fucking boyfriend," he said, looking at Bruce, "of your son's."

"Don't worry, Darcy Warcy, we've taken care of that. Unfortunately, your laptop burned in the fire, along with all those pretty pictures. And you tell that cow to stop her mooing. Be a man and stand up to the bitch."

Darcy nodded. "The coach's house burned to the ground. Fire Department called him."

"Enough of that. Son," He looked at Bruce. "Do you know that Darcy here enjoys being whipped, especially his dick, while he's being fucked?"

Darcy looked embarrassed.

"Would you like my handsome son to give you your lesson tonight, Darcy, or do you want to watch him give it to the pretty boy?"

Bruce stiffened in his chair, his eyes widening as Darcy went to his knees and laid his head on the man's shoe. "Both, please, Bruce, both."

CHAPTER FIFTEEN

"How many other fucking pieces of garbage are there out there besides you?"

Joe stood outside the door as August placed the phonebook against Desmond's face again and punched it hard.

Desmond tried to fend off the blows. "Jesus Christ, August, I told you that you already know. Darcy French, that's all . . . and the coach, Richardson, but only pictures and stuff."

"And you."

"I never participated. I swear to God."

"You protected them. There had to be something in it for you."

"Sometimes I . . . I watched, that's all. Just the sex, I never . . . never . . . murdered anyone. I don't know anything about that."

August hit him again. "You filthy pig."

When he'd recovered from that blow, Desmond gave him a faint smile. "That phonebook shit doesn't work. Eventually, you'll break the blood vessels. They'll nab you for police brutality. I'll walk away from this."

"You won't fucking walk anywhere. You tried to kill me. And, right now, I don't give a shit what they do to me. This feels too good. So, keep on lying, and I'm going to keep on hitting. You protected those fucks. You watched them molest and murder innocent children."

"It was only the movies. I . . . enjoyed the movies."

"You enjoyed the movies. They filmed it all, didn't they?"

"Darcy mainly. He's a computer geek. Then they'd go to Richardson's house and watch it in the basement on the big screen. No one died until your fucking boyfriend came to town. He brought evil with him."

August grabbed Desmond's shirt and pulled him forward. "What evil? I want to know who he is. And I want to know where in the hell Alice is, and Bruce, and that Ludlow kid."

"I . . . I don't know." He shook his head, his eyes filled with fear as August picked up the phone book. "I told them that I wasn't into any heavy stuff. I didn't want to know about . . . I didn't want any part of murdering that boy."

"But you let it go. French and Richardson know who the murderer is, and so do you."

"You don't want to know." He shook his head.

"August . . ."

August moved around back of Desmond and wrapped his arm around his throat. "Tell me, or I'll snap your neck like a twig. Do it, Desmond. Tell me who he is and where that Ludlow kid is. Do it now. You have five seconds . . . Five, four, three—" Desmond nodded.

August released him and waited for Desmond to recover his breath. "The old . . ." He coughed. "The old Edwards cottage, the one that was back in the woods. It—"

"Who is he, the one who killed my little brother?" August hollered, his foot kicking Desmond's chair, almost knocking him over. "Who is he?"

"B-bruce M-Monkton," he stammered.

"You're fucking playing with me now. I'll . . ." August took his revolver out of his holster and pointed it at Desmond's head.

"No, really, please, August," he begged. "It is Bruce Monkton, the father, not the son. The father!"

August lowered his gun, his jaw dropping. "He signed

his real name," he whispered to himself. "Why didn't Bruce tell me? I knew his father left when he was young, but . . . he must have blanked it out somehow."

August looked at Joe, suddenly snapping back to the present. He reloaded his gun. "I want all the names of all the other creeps in town that are into this child pornography ring. And if Monkton has a gang of rats in this town, he must have them in other places where these boys showed up dead years ago. Don't let this prick sleep," He hooked his thumb at Desmond. "Until you get a complete list of names, and then round them up, one by one."

Joe nodded. "Yes, sir."

"Backup will be here from Manchester soon. Let them know where I am. Fill in the officer in charge." August headed to the door.

"August, don't go out there alone," Desmond hollered after him. "He'll kill you!"

"I need a drink," Bruce said, turning his attention away from Darcy French's embarrassing display on the floor.

"Darcy, pet," Monkton said, "get me and the boy here a drink." He tilted his head at Bruce as Darcy scrambled to pour drinks at the bar. "So, Bruce, what was it like, sex with that big stud?"

Bruce swallowed. He'd never disclose the intimate details of his sex life with August to this fiend. "Fantastic," he said lightly. He closed his eyes a moment. Making love with August had been heaven, feeling his body close to his, inside of him, and sometimes the sex had been rough and kinky, but always loving. He wouldn't cry. The tears were over. He had a job to do—to kill this bastard before anything happened to that boy—and he was going to do it.

"Ever do leather?"

"Sure." He shrugged.

"Tied him up?"

"You bet," he said lightly.

"Fucked him until he couldn't stand it anymore then strangled him until the light went out of his eyes?"

Bruce swallowed, trying not focus on his insanity. "Didn't get around to that."

"Too late now."

Bruce nodded.

"I'm sorry, son. He had to go, but I guarantee you there will be other pleasures in store."

Darcy had set the drinks in front of them, two large glasses of whiskey.

"Drink up," his father said. "Bliss is waiting in the other room. We'll get rid of him in the morning and blow this place. What do you say?"

"Good idea."

"We've outstayed our welcome." He winked and took a swallow of his whiskey.

"And what about me?" Darcy whined.

"You'll go on viewing your snuff films and jerking off to your pictures of five-year-olds. I have other people waiting for me in other towns, Darcy. I'm not yours exclusively."

"Of course." He went back to the floor.

"You want him naked?" he asked Bruce.

"No, I mean, he's not really my type."

"I know, but you can do anything you like. He welcomes it, don't you, little dog?" Monkton reached down between French's legs and squeezed his testicles brutally.

Bruce winced when the man cried out in pain.

"See? You want more, Darcy?" Darcy French nodded.

Fuck. Bruce remembered peeking through the slats in the closet to see his father standing over Clay as he was stretched out on the bed. The belt hit him between the legs several times as he cried, and then his father hovered over him, unzipping his pants as he flipped Clay over on the bed, smacking him with the belt. "Time to give Daddy a ride," he'd said with a laugh.

Bruce had stopped looking then. He'd covered his ears and hidden his face in the corner of the dark closet. *Make it stop. Make it stop. Make it stop.* All this time, he'd been running from a killer and running from the man who'd sexually abused both him and Clay when they were obscenely young. *A monster. My father is a monster. What does that make me?*

When they rose from the table, Darcy French being forced to crawl on his knees in front of them, Bruce reached out and grabbed the poker as he passed the fireplace. He gripped it in his hand, ready to strike as the man in front of him turned around and looked at him.

Bruce put it behind him.

"Walk in front of me," his father said. "I don't want you to get lost."

Bruce quickly switched the poker to the front. When Darcy went to look up at him, he barked, "No one fucking told you to turn around. Keep crawling, worm." He didn't need either one of them to spot the poker in his hand.

"That's it," his father said from behind him. "You got the hang of it now."

August drove like a bat out of hell, only slowing down once to see Coach Richardson being put into a squad car by two officers Joe had sent out to his house, or what was left of it. He made it out to the lake in half the usual time, slowing down as he passed his old house and stopping. He'd walk the rest of the way. He knew it well.

He'd go through the path in the woods and around back. *Please, Bruce. Please be alright.*

August shone a flashlight to the ground as he pushed past

the trees. He glanced around him. He could see the moon-light shining down on Blood Pond, making it shimmer and look almost alive somehow. When he saw something that looked like a log up ahead, he slowed his pace, his heart in his throat. It wasn't a log. He knew that. He could smell something like the scent of rotting meat. Was it the Ludlow kid, his head in the pond already? Was it Alice? Oh God, maybe it was . . . Bruce? No, he couldn't handle that right now. He approached slowly, his heart pounding in his chest, his gun clenched in his hand. He retched when he saw the remains of what had to be the Jameson boy. "Jesus Christ."

They had searched these woods thoroughly when the head had been found in the pond. They would have found the body. Someone had dumped the rest of that kid here after keeping it somewhere else a while. He retched again and covered his nose.

He kept moving. There was nothing he could do for that poor boy now. He looked around cautiously, ready to shoot and ask questions later. He could see the house now, just beyond the trees from where he stood. There was a light burning through the dining room window and a stack of boxes piled on the front porch. He quickly crossed the lawn and crept around the side to the back. There were lights there too and a small porch with a few stairs leading to the back door. There was no basement. He looked around for vehicles and noticed a car and a motorcycle parked on the other side of the house, hidden by trees. Tire tracks indicated that someone had left recently, someone driving a 4x4, which is what Coach Richardson drove.

He knew realistically that he should wait for backup, but there was no time. This maniac had Bruce and the Ludlow kid in there.

August quietly climbed the steps to the porch. Carefully he turned the door handle, holding his breath until he realized that it was unlocked. He slipped inside and quietly closed the door behind him.

He moved noiselessly down the carpeted hallway, voices now coming to his ear. One of them was definitely Bruce. His gun poised, he stopped dead when he heard Bruce say, "I really like them this age, so young and tight."

August frowned. He was startled to hear that come out of Bruce's mouth. Why in hell was he talking like that?

"We're going to make such a good team," another voice replied, an older voice, calm, confident. "Take off the gag. Let me show you how to make him scream."

August didn't wait any longer. He swung around the corner, gun drawn, and found himself staring at Bruce.

"Thank God, August," Bruce cried out. "You're alive."

An older man with a great resemblance to Bruce stood behind him, blond and handsome, a charming smile on his face. He had one arm wrapped around Bruce's shoulder from behind, casually crossing his throat. Desmond couldn't see what was in his hand or if he had anything in the other hand.

The gesture looked innocent enough, a father hugging his son, but August knew it was anything but.

There was a body lying on a table behind them. He could see the bindings on the feet. Beyond them was an open window. The lace curtain was flapping gently in the breeze.

A small voice came from behind the table, and a naked man with fogged-up glasses crawled out on his knees. "Please," he begged, "don't kill me."

"Who in the fuck are you?" August demanded.

"Darcy French. I . . . please . . ." He began to sob.

"Get over there in the corner and shut up," August told him.

"Sorry, I forgot to take out the pet," Bruce Monkton smirked.

"Get your hands up now, Monkton, and let him go," August barked, the gun aimed at the man's forehead.

"Now, August," he said, tilting his head, "is that any way to treat your father-in-law?"

"You're not my fucking father-in-law. Let Bruce go and get your hands up."

"He's free to go," he said, lifting his hands and then instantly grabbing Bruce again. This time a knife with a twelve-inch, stainless steel blade was poised at Bruce's throat. "He can go to hell and so can you," he said softly, pressing the blade to Bruce's throat.

"Don't hurt him," August said.

He shrugged. "What goes around comes around. Let me go, and I'll give you back your precious fucked up boy."

"Shoot him!" Bruce cried out. "Shoot him, August!"

"Shut up, loser." The man pressed the knife harder, drawing blood now. "Or I'll take your head off. What a high that would be."

"Fucking shoot him!" Bruce cried out.

"Shoot me, and I'll take off his head right here, right now," he threatened.

"Never mind me. Kill him, kill the son of —"

The knife sliced through the flesh of Bruce's throat and August fired off a shot.

Bruce fell, clutching his throat, and Monkton turned and jumped out the window.

August went to Bruce. "Are you alright?" Bruce nodded and got to his feet.

August looked down at the floor and saw the blood. He had hit Monkton, but it must have only been a graze. He'd been so afraid of hitting Bruce.

He spotted a towel on the counter and handed it to Bruce. "Hold this to the wound." He grabbed his phone and punched in 911. "Get an ambulance out here to forty-five

Lake Road and patch me into the local police station." August checked the pulse on the Ludlow kid as he briefly filled Joe in on what was happening.

"Thank God, he's alive." Bruce swallowed.

"Manchester police are twenty minutes away," Joe said on the other end of the line. "Get that son of a bitch, August."

Bruce was holding the towel to his throat now, but he was standing. "I'll look after the kid," he said as August tucked his phone back into his pocket then looked at Darcy French. "And that creep. He won't be any trouble, will he?" Bruce asked.

August walked over, grabbed one of French's arms and handcuffed him to the leg of the heavy wooden sideboard that stood in the corner. "He won't be now. Look," August said, "the police are going to be crawling all over this place in about a half hour. Tell them to take the laptop out of the back seat of my car. It belongs to that shithead there." He looked over at French, who was sobbing. "He's got it all on film."

"I'll tell them. August," Bruce said, grabbing his arm, "be careful."

August walked to the door.

"Get the fucking bastard."

August winked at him then raced out of the house.

Bruce cried bitter tears as he undid the ropes that bound Peter Ludlow. He found a blanket and covered him up. The boy was stunned, a little groggy from some drug he'd been given, but he was going to be alright.

Bruce hugged the boy tightly, so grateful that he was alive. "I wouldn't have let them hurt you," he whispered, feeling a little lightheaded from the loss of blood.

"Is it . . . going to be . . . am I okay?"

"Yes," Bruce said, "you're okay. You're going home. Just stay here, stay put." He walked to the window. In the distance, he could see just the corner of Blood Pond. All around him were trees. *August. Please. Finish this once and for all and come back.* He couldn't expect to be with August anymore, not with everything that had happened. And the abuse had come back to his memories, so vivid and painful he doubted he'd be able to deal with all this without help.

He thought about Clay as he placed his hand on the Ludlow kid's shoulder. Clay had taken most of the beatings and sexual violations, sometimes pretending that he was Bruce and taking it twice . . . until finally something in his mind just snapped. Maybe Evelyn coped as best she could. The father of her children had been a madman, and she'd been too terrified to tell anyone. And all these years, Bruce guessed, his father had continued to terrorize her.

He knew what it meant to live in fear, and as the tears flowed, he knew what love was now, real love, the love August had given him, even when Bruce hadn't made it easy for him. To love one person the way he loved August was the greatest gift he'd ever had. But he couldn't continue to ruin the man's life. It wasn't fair that August be stuck with a fuckup like him, but did he love his man enough to let him go?

August didn't know if Monkton had a gun. He had a knife sharp enough to decapitate someone. That was enough if Monkton snuck up on him.

The man was insane but bright. Most serial killers were. They feared nothing, laughed in these situations, so sure they'd win. August had studied enough of them to know that most had been damaged in their youth, tortured animals as kids, and, after their first kill, got high from the thrill of the next one.

Monkton had his own following, his own cult members, and even if they weren't all murderers, they worshipped at the same demented altar, children in servitude, sexually exploited and used for the pleasure of sexually immature monsters.

His senses were on high alert, and perspiration dotted his forehead. He listened for every little sound. He couldn't mess this one up. He had to get him. It had been so long coming. He could taste it now, the adrenaline flowing through his veins. All he could think about was Tommy and how this was for him, as well as all the others.

He stopped suddenly when he heard the cracking of a twig somewhere. At first, he hadn't been sure if he'd taken the right direction. He knew Monkton was on foot and had fled through the woods. He had left the motorcycle, and the car belonging to Darcy French was still there.

August had followed his instincts, thinking that Monkton would head for the main highway where maybe he could hitch a ride out of town. The cracking of that twig, although it might have been a wolf or a lynx, gave him some hope that he wasn't far behind him. He had an advantage. Monkton had at least ten years on him, and August worked out regularly. He was in great shape, and he could run fast when he had to. He wasn't going to give up until he hunted this killer down and put an end to him. He didn't want to even think about what he'd do when he got his hands on him.

The flashlight was directed toward the ground as he scanned the terrain, looking for any tracks. He spotted a man's fresh footprint suddenly and looked up to see something move in the bushes. August took off in that direction, heading into the bush on a run.

In the distance, he caught a glimpse of blond hair through

the trees. August doubled his pace, half tripping over brush. Police sirens were now wailing in the distance, and August looked around helplessly, feeling dwarfed by the huge trees. For a moment, he thought he'd lost him, then he realized that Monkton had abruptly double-backed and now was running in the other direction. Monkton had heard the sirens too, and August knew where he was going. He was headed for Blood Pond.

August was breathing hard as he ran, but he had no intention of slowing down. He was this close. He could taste it. *Tommy. He's going to pay, little brother. I promise you, kid.*

When he reached the edge of the woods, he stood, bending a bit to try and catch his breath. The answer to whether Monkton had a gun was suddenly answered when a shot fired and hit a tree right beside his head. August dropped to the ground for a moment, crawling forward on his belly. He peered through the trees and saw a figure running down the embankment toward the water. August got to his feet and scrambled after him. He fired a shot in the air, but Monkton was too far away. The threat of a gunshot wouldn't stop him now. He had too much to lose. August knew just what his plans were. It's exactly what he'd do in his situation. Monkton was going to swim across Blood Pond and take a shorter route to the highway before the roadblocks went up.

The man had already dived into the pond when August got to the water. He could see that Monkton was halfway across the pond already. It was a gamble going in after him because his gun would probably be useless, but he had no choice. He dove in and started to swim as if his life depended on it. One swift, strong stroke followed another, his respiration coming fast and hard. He couldn't think about the pain.

Bruce stood in front of the house. He scanned the horizon as two local police officers carted Darcy French off in the squad car. Joe was there, fawning a bit over him, suggesting that he get an officer to drive him back to the hotel if he wouldn't go to the hospital.

"I'm not going anywhere until August comes back," Bruce told him.

Joe had already had the laptop retrieved from August's car and was busy talking to the big boys from Manchester who'd just arrived.

Bruce allowed the medic to bandage his throat and made sure they took care of Peter Ludlow. They kept suggesting that he go to the hospital, but the wound wasn't life-threatening.

The Manchester police were all over the place now, lights flashing and evidence people dusting for fingerprints. A police officer from August's department that Bruce had met before came over to him as soon as he noticed him. "Bruce. Are you alright?"

"David, right?"

"Yes, David Zeniki."

"I'm okay."

He nodded. "Good."

"August went after him, Bruce Monkton, my father. He's the one who's been killing all these boys, even those boys in other parts of the state."

"We know," he said, placing a hand on his shoulder. "It's a hard thing to find out that it's your father."

"I didn't remember him, but then I did. Don't feel sorry for me. I have no love for this man. Please just find August, okay?"

"We're going to find August," Zeniki assured him.

Then he started barking orders to everyone.

Monkton tried to climb out of Blood Pond several times, but August dragged him back into the water. August's only thought was that he wanted to kill this bastard. It didn't really matter how he did it. They struggled in the water, punching, and wrestling, while Monkton desperately tried to get away. They were both worn down from the chase.

August took him around the throat and tightened his hold, one hand trying to keep Monkton from reaching inside his waistband where August knew he had stashed the knife.

When August saw the glint of steel in the water, he knew Monkton had managed to get his hands on the knife. He sprang away from him and yelped as the knife ripped through his upper thigh. The pain was intense. The knife was still in Monkton's hand ready to strike again.

It wasn't deep around the edge of the pond, and the water was quite cold tonight. Monkton easily made his way toward him through the shallow water, knife poised in his hand. "I don't think I like the idea of you fucking my little boy." He gritted his teeth, a sinister smile on his face. "That's my job, cop!"

"Fucking prick." August lunged for him. His foot encountered something in the water, and he fell forward, floating for a second.

Monkton danced away with a laugh, and August looked down to see two dead eyes staring up at him. He yelled and swam backwards. "Oh no, Alice, no." He shook his head, stunned for a moment, as if he'd been hit with something then realized that Monkton was wading toward the bank again.

August dove for Monkton, grabbing a fistful of that blond hair, and yanked him backwards hard. "It's over!" he shouted. Monkton struggled in the water as August pushed him under and scrambled to grab the knife.

Suddenly August felt the handle of the knife in his hand.

As he looked down at the face in the water, he saw that Monkton was smiling. August brought the knife down into Monkton's chest with every ounce of strength he had left. Bubbles came up to the surface of Blood Pond as August held Monkton under. Blood pooled out around them, creating a cloud around Monkton's head as August bore down with the knife, gritting his teeth hard.

"August. Stop"

The water moved around him. Someone grabbed his arm from behind as his hand raised in the air, the knife dripping with Monkton's blood, poised to strike again.

David Zeniki held him back as two other officers dragged Monkton up onto the bank and began to give him artificial respiration. "He's still alive," someone cried out.

"Let him die!" August screamed out. "Let the bastard die." He was struggling as David held him fast.

"August, August, you got him. You got him, buddy."

August turned and looked at David. "He killed my brother. He killed Alice. Jesus, she's here." He pointed to the water. "In Blood Pond."

"Oh no." David's face paled.

"I want to kill him. Why don't you let me kill him?"

"Because you're not yourself right now, August."

"I'm more myself than I've ever been." He looked over as the medics arrived with a stretcher. "It would have given me satisfaction to leave his head in Blood Pond."

"Then you'd be just like him," David replied.

"No." August shook his head and watched as they lifted Monkton onto the stretcher. "I'd have a good reason. He never had one." He met David's gaze.

David nodded and released him.

They started to slowly wade out of the pond.

"You need to go to the hospital. Your leg is bleeding badly, August."

The ambulance doors closed. "I want a cop on his door at all times, you understand me?"

David nodded. "He'll be well guarded. He's not going anywhere. I promise."

August nodded, and then he collapsed on the grass.

Bruce was relieved to see August open his eyes. "Hey, beautiful," he whispered. He was so happy to see August again, to know that he was alright.

August reached for his hand. Bruce took it and held it in his. "You okay?" August asked.

"I am now. They insisted on doing some stuff to me when I came back with you. I'll be fine. The cut wasn't deep enough to cause any damage. You got him."

August looked away.

"What? August?"

"I wanted to kill him. If I'd had my way, he'd be dead."

"He won't be able to hurt anyone anymore."

August met his gaze, but he didn't say anything. The disappointment on his face literally felt painful to Bruce.

"I have something I need to tell you." Bruce lowered his head a minute. He wasn't sure how he was going to say the words, but he had to say them.

"What is it?"

"I'm going to go away for a while." Bruce saw something cross August's face, pain, confusion. Bruce swallowed hard.

"I don't understand. Why?" August asked. "You're leaving me?"

There was silence. Bruce moved away. He walked to the other side of the room. If he didn't put some distance between them, he wouldn't be able to say it. "I love you, August, I love you too much, but I can't ruin your life."

"Ruin my life? How in the hell have you ruined my life? I

love you."

Bruce's eyes filled with tears. He couldn't speak as his throat seemed to close, choking him. "I'm . . . sorry," he managed to choke out and ran from the room.

August tried to sit up, but he couldn't because he was hooked up to every tube going. "Goddamn it."

A few hours later, David walked into the hospital room. "They're pushing Monkton's arraignment up to two weeks from now. It's going to be a long trial. He'll be in the prison hospital until then. He's in bad shape. He might not make it."

"One can only hope."

"We've got enough, with that laptop of French's, to put him and half the town away with him. How are you doing? Doctor says you've lost a lot of blood, but you'll be fine."

"He's got to die."

"He probably will get the death penalty; it's capital murder."

"David, no one has been executed in this state since nineteen-thirty-nine. We don't even have a death chamber, and there's been one person on death row since two-thousand and eight."

"I thought you were against the death penalty. You told me it discriminated against the poor."

"It does. I hate it, but Monkton is not just a criminal. He's evil incarnate. And he'll find a way to get out and murder again."

"We'll do our best to make sure that doesn't happen."

"After it goes to court, it's out of our hands."

"August," David said, touching his shoulder, "I know this is personal for you on many levels but —"

"My brother was murdered by him, my former partner was murdered by him, and now my lover is leaving me because his father is a monster who destroyed him. Not to mention, how many other boys has he tortured and murdered?"

"Three here and seven upstate."

"That we know of."

"Bruce will change his mind about leaving you."

August knew it had taken a lot for David to say that. His sexuality was usually either not mentioned by other cops on the force or subjected to the occasional bad joke. "I appreciate the sentiment, but, no, he won't change his mind." August struggled to sit up. "I've got to get out of here."

CHAPTER SIXTEEN

Two months later

His neighbor was standing outside on the porch calling her cat when August pulled up in the driveway. He got out, and she waved at him. "Hi, August."

She was a nice elderly lady who always referred to Bruce as his gentleman friend.

"Hello, Mrs. Irons."

"I'm so sorry to see a for sale sign on the house." She came down off her veranda. "I felt real safe having a policeman next door. Any buyers?"

"Not yet. The market isn't good."

"That gentleman friend of yours not coming back?"

"Doesn't seem like it," he said with a tight smile.

"You look tired, August. Long shifts lately?"

She didn't miss anything. He'd been taking a lot of overtime just to fill up the empty hours. "Yes," he said. "I'm off tomorrow though. I'm going to sleep."

"Good. I see that killer's trial is still going on. He's going to be convicted, isn't he?"

"We hope so," he said.

"I didn't know your brother was killed. I'm sorry."

He nodded. He didn't want to be rude, but he really didn't want to talk about that. He'd had a lot of bad dreams lately, and he was taking anti-depressants again, hoping the department didn't find out. The trial had taken a toll, not to mention all the time he'd spent on his testimony. Bruce, too, had been asked to testify in the proceedings, but it was rare that they were in the courtroom as the same time. At the most, he'd seen him from a distance.

Finally, August managed to get away from the neighbor and went inside. Bruce had sent him a few emails during the trial, but August didn't know where he was staying. August had suggested selling the house, and Bruce never answered, so he wrote back and said he'd give him half if he sold it. Still no answer.

He lay back on the sofa and closed his eyes. He dreamed of Bruce, that he came into his bedroom. He was naked, and he looked like an angel. "August, I miss you so much."

August opened his arms. Bruce was touching him, kissing him, moving his mouth over his hard sex. August massaged his erection, moaned softly. "Bruce," he whispered. "Baby."

The phone woke him out of his dream. He swore, reached over onto the end table and picked it up. "Hello?" He looked at the clock on the wall. It was after ten.

Dead air. August hung up and checked his caller ID. Restricted.

The phone rang again. He thought maybe it was Bruce. Maybe he wanted to come home, but he didn't know how to say it. "Bruce?"

The phone clicked off.

He stood up, paced his living room then looked out the window. He took out his cell phone and called the precinct. He got David. "Is Bruce Monkton still being held here in Manchester?"

"Where else would he be?"

"Find out."

"August, you're being paranoid."

"Find out!" He hung up and went back to the window.

When the phone rang again, August picked up and said, "You fucking bastard, this time, I'm going to finish you."

He listened, then he heard a voice say, "You gotta find me first."

August slammed the phone down repeatedly until the plastic receiver cracked in half.

His cell phone rang.

"August," David said, breathing hard. "He's out, killed two guards about an hour ago. We got an all-points bulletin out and—"

"Find his son and put him under police protection," August demanded and hung up. He went to his computer and wrote Bruce an email. He had no idea if he'd see it. He wrote simply.

Bruce. Call the police. He's out. Don't worry. I'm going to finish it this time. Be careful. I still love you.

August reloaded his gun and grabbed his jacket and his keys. He called the precinct again. "I want to be informed the minute Bruce Monkton is spotted, you understand? The moment."

David came on the line. "August, listen, don't do anything rash before—"

August got into his car and started the engine. "Nothing matters, David, not my job, not my life. The only thing that matters is that I find this bastard and I kill him. Wrong or right, he's going to die. Don't call me again unless you have him in your sights." He hung up.

August knew exactly where to go. He parked his car on a side street near Maple. Here were the gay bars, and the under-aged male prostitutes. Monkton was going to take another, and since he couldn't hang around the schools at this time of night, this is where he'd come, to stalk for victims near the gay bars. August stood and watched the customers negotiate blowjobs across the street.

He was perfectly calm for some reason. He'd somehow known this was going to happen. It was meant to be. He took out a cigarette and lit it. With no one to discipline him, he'd taken it up again after Bruce left. He sucked some smoke into his lungs and waited.

When one of the young boys from across the street spotted him, he walked over, probably thinking August was too shy to approach.

"Hey, baby, I'll do you for ten."

August opened his coat and flashed his badge.

"Shit," he said. He'd turned, ready to bolt, when August reached out and grabbed his arm.

"No worries. I'm looking for someone."

"Oh. Who?"

"A blond guy, handsome, in his forties, big smile, charming."

"Haven't seen anyone like that."

"If someone wanted to find real young boys, like . . . fourteen or under, where would they go?"

"I can't tell you that." He smiled. "You into young meat?"

"Listen, if you tell me where I can find your pimp, I'll give you a hundred."

"I want to live, man."

"I promise I won't say you told me, won't even say I'm a cop. I just want to find this guy who'd be interested in that."

"My pimp is at the Glory Rider." He pointed then opened his palm.

August took out the money. "What's his name?"

"Harry. He's an Italian with a scar down his left cheek. You'll know when you see him. He runs a stable out of the back door of the club, two alleys down."

August gave him the bill and walked down the street.

Ten minutes later, he had the place. He saw the pimp by the name of Harry, a huge scar down the side of his face, not exactly a looker, standing in the alley.

August lit another cigarette and walked down the alley.

"Harry?"

The stubby little rat looked at him.

"You got young meat here?"

He put up his hands. "I don't know what you're talking about."

August grabbed the front of his silky shirt and backed him against the wall.

"Hey!"

"Listen, I'm not looking to arrest your ass today, so consider yourself lucky. Answer my questions, and you'll walk."

"How young we talking?"

"Young. You got boys ten, eleven, babies?"

"Sure. If you've got the money, you can get any kind of meat."

"Had any customers so far tonight?"

"Night is young."

"Night is over. Get lost. I'm filling in for now."

Harry said nothing when August released him. He just hurried off down the alley. When the door opened, and a young boy poked his head out, August told him to go back inside. He pulled the hood of his sweatshirt over his head and did up his leather jacket then he leaned against the wall and waited.

When his cell phone rang, he didn't answer. He received an email a few seconds later saying they hadn't found Bruce Monkton yet. Nothing from Bruce. He sighed.

He hoped he got the message. If Monkton laid one hand on Bruce . . .

Less than an hour later, he spotted a figure in the distance. He was talking to someone, and they were pointing down the alley. August wasn't sure it was Monkton until he got halfway. Then he was sure, and the adrenaline started to pump. August stepped out into the alley, gun drawn. "Hello, Bruce," he said.

Bruce placed his hand into his pocket, and August fired off one shot. It hit him right in the forehead, and he went down onto one knee then dropped forward, face first. August walked over to where he lay and looked at him. He kicked him with the toe of his boot then went down on his knee and checked his pulse. He couldn't find one. Bruce Monkton was dead. He patted him down just to be sure and found a gun. He left it there, knowing that Monkton had his fingers on it before August pulled the trigger.

August got to his feet and called the precinct. "I found Bruce Monkton. He had a gun. He tried to draw it, and I fired. We need a body bag." He hung up.

He lit another cigarette and stood there, leaning against the building "You wanted me, Monkton, you found me. You just couldn't leave it alone. That was lucky for me." He took another couple of puffs and threw the cigarette away. He was quitting.

A few hours later, August was sitting in the interrogation room. An officer was reading his statement back to him. "Are you ready to sign it?" he asked.

"That's what happened." He took the form and scrawled his name on it.

The inspector from Internal Affairs checked it over and nodded. "Everything seems in order; we found the weapon. The only question I have is how you knew he'd go there."

"I didn't really. I just guessed. He was a compulsive sort of guy. Killing was a high for him, and he needed it. I knew that's the first thing he'd do, plus he wanted to pay me back. He had to get one up again. What better way than to kill?"

"I guess it's over."

"No," August said, "he's got followers all over the place

into kiddie porn and torture. We need to go where he's travelled and track down these people."

"That's a job for another department."

"I want out of homicide. I've seen enough of this stuff."

"But you're good, August, we can't lose you."

August stood up. "I'm finished, Martin."

"What will you do?"

He thought about that for a few minutes. "Maybe private investigation, finding missing children. At least out of homicide, I'll probably find a few alive occasionally." Martin nodded, and August left the room.

When he walked out into the squad room, his eyes widened. Bruce was there on the bench. He got to his feet when August came out.

"Bruce?"

Bruce walked over to him. "You okay? I heard what happened."

"You got my email."

Bruce nodded. "Yes. And the cops picked me up and brought me here for safekeeping. Can we get out of here now, talk?"

"Yeah. Sure."

They walked together for a while down the street. Bruce seemed to be looking for his words.

"What did you want to tell me?" August asked, his stomach in knots. They stopped in front of a park.

"I don't want to sell the house, August."

"I do. I don't want to stay here anymore. I'm leaving the department, Bruce. I'm going to find something else to do. I can't do this anymore."

Bruce nodded. "Is he really dead?"

"Yes."

"Good."

They started to walk again. "You know I was prepared to

go with him, to play along so that I could protect Peter Ludlow. Then I planned to kill him when I had the chance."

"If he didn't kill you first. I'm glad it never came to that."

"He tortured Clay as a child, and Clay took it for me. That's why he was the way he was, and I think Clay thought I owed him for that. I went to talk to someone about all this stuff, and they told me that none of it is my fault. Deep down I know that, but . . . August . . ." Bruce looked into his eyes. "You're the only one who can make me feel as if my life counts for something. I figure if you love me, I can't be all bad."

"Bruce," August replied with a sigh. "Oh, Bruce, you're not bad at all." He looked down at him. "You've just had a shitty life."

Bruce smiled sadly. "I tried to stay away from you. I thought I'd fucked your life up enough, starting with Tommy. But I . . ." He swallowed. "God, I love you, August. I can't help it, although I tried to stop. You're the only good thing that's ever happened to me. You know?" The tears flowed down his face. "That's damn hard to let go."

"Yes, Goddamn it, it is," August replied, his voice hoarse with emotion, "and you don't have to let go of it. Don't ever let go of me, Bruce."

Bruce went into his arms, and August held him for a few minutes. Then he kissed Bruce's hair and released him. "Let's leave this place, baby, make a fresh start somewhere else, put all of this behind us for good this time. I never want to come back here again. I want to get as far away from Blood Pond as I possibly can, right out of the state. No more death. Just life, and love, you loving me. Oh God, Bruce, I've missed you. I almost lost my mind thinking you didn't want me anymore."

Bruce touched August's cheek. He reached up and pressed his mouth tenderly to his, and that was all the answer they would ever need.

The End

ABOUT THE AUTHOR

I write not only for my own pleasure but for the pleasure of my readers. I can't remember a time in my life when I haven't written and told stories. When I'm not writing, I'm dreaming about writing, doing something wild and adventurous, or trying to make the world a better and more open-minded place to live in. I adore beautiful men, and I know I'm not alone in this! Eroticism between consenting adults, in all its many forms, is the icing on the cake of life!

D.J. has published well over two hundred novels/novellas and is a well-seasoned writer.

www.ingramcontent.com/pod-product-compliance
Lightning Source LLC
Chambersburg PA
CBHW060613130626
46555CB00002B/513